SMOLDERING DESIRE

HELLFIRE BOOK #3

ELLE JAMES

TWISTED PAGE INC

SMOLDERING DESIRE

HELLFIRE SERIES BOOK #3

New York Times & *USA Today*
Bestselling Author

ELLE JAMES

This book is dedicated to first responders who risk their lives to save others' lives. Their selflessness speaks of their desire to help others in their times of need.

Escape with...

Elle James

aka Myla Jackson

AUTHOR'S NOTE

Enjoy other books in the HELLFIRE Series
by Elle James

Hellfire Series
Hellfire, Texas (#1)
Justice Burning (#2)
Smoldering Desire (#3)
Hellfire in High Heels (#4)
Playing With Fire (#5) TBD
Up in Flames (#6) TBD
Total Meltdown (#7) TBD

Visit ellejames.com for more titles and release dates
For hot cowboys, visit her alter ego Myla Jackson at
mylajackson.com
and join Elle James and Myla Jackson's Newsletter at
Newsletter

CHAPTER 1

THE LONG RIDE in the country, on curvy roads with stunning views of the Texas blue bonnets in full bloom, did nothing to cool the anger burning in Rider Grayson's gut. His ex-wife didn't know when to quit. He'd given her everything in their divorce. The house, her car, their membership at the exclusive Dallas country club and the entire contents of their savings.

And she wanted more.

The letter he'd received in the mail that morning from her attorney had made him so mad he'd locked up his shop, hopped on his Harley and hit the road. The woman had taken everything in their marriage and had never contributed toward their happiness. Why should he give her anything else?

Rider should have known better than to marry a Dallas debutante. He'd been so caught up in climbing the corporate ladder and making a name for himself in high finance, he'd lost himself. Marrying Lydia Farnsworth had ultimately reminded him of his roots and what was important. Not the fancy cars or hobnobbing in the wealthiest of social circles or kissing up to the most influential individuals in the state.

Family was more important than any of that. And the ability to look in the mirror and like who he saw. Thus, his ultimatum and subsequent move back to Hellfire, Texas. In his heart, he'd known what Lydia would choose. She'd been the product of her upbringing. Private schools, the best of the best social circles and everything her daddy's money could buy her. Why would she choose to move to his hometown of Hellfire when she had everything her heart desired in Dallas?

When she'd refused to move with him, the decision to divorce had come easy. The reality of the legal ramifications had taken a lot longer. Over a year and tens of thousands of dollars in legal fees and, finally, he was free. He'd purchased the garage he'd been leasing and started his life over. Then the letter from Lydia's attorney had jerked him back into the nightmare.

As he entered his hometown, he finally slowed, willing himself to relax. No one here had set out to make him mad. They didn't deserve the brunt of his anger. Every street, every house and storefront was as familiar to Rider as the ranch he'd grown up on with his three brothers and sister. He let that feeling of home and belonging wash over him.

Before he headed back to his shop, he needed to get fuel for his ride. He wondered if Selena was working the gas station and convenience store that day. She always had a smile on her face. He could use one right then. It might improve his mood.

Rider pulled into the Gas-N-Go, the only station in town, and parked his motorcycle in front of one of the service pumps. When he swung his leg over the seat and stood, he was reminded of how long he'd been burning off steam and how many years it had been since he'd ridden anything, motorcycle or horse, for an extended period. The muscles of his inner thighs twinged. He took a moment to work out the kinks before unscrewing the cap off the tank and placing the pump nozzle inside.

Once the gas started flowing into his tank, he glanced through the window of the store, his gaze going to the sable-haired beauty standing at the counter, her brown eyes shining, a smile spreading across her lush, full lips.

He was still amazed at how much Selena Sanchez, the ranch foreman's daughter, had grown up from the little girl with pigtails, who used to follow him and his brothers and sister around the ranch. In what seemed like an overnight transformation, she'd gone from a gangly teen to this well-rounded, confident young woman managing a store. Well, maybe not overnight. Rider had been in Dallas for a few years. But, *damn*.

The woman was as different from Lydia as a jungle was to a dry, West Texas desert. Lydia was beautiful, but her lips were thin, like her model-thin figure. Her smile only seemed to turn on when a camera was pointed in her direction.

Selena had lush written in every cell of her body, from her warm skin tones to her well-rounded curves. And it wasn't as if she worked on being all that sexy. The woman just was. On top of that, she had a personality that lit up a room. Selena smiled for everyone, and even when no one else was around.

And, at that moment, she was smiling at him.

Her cheerfulness could have irritated him, but not today. He needed her little ray of sunshine to get him back on track, and on to the work he needed to accomplish that day.

When the tank was full, he replaced the nozzle on the pump, screwed the cap on the tank and pushed the bike to a parking place in front of the store. He might as well grab a cup of coffee while he was there. Selena always had a fresh pot brewing with anything better than he could make on his own. His shop was across the street and less than a block away.

A truckload of Hispanic construction workers pulled into the convenience store parking lot and six men clambered out, all speaking Spanish, laughing and joking.

Rider gave them half a glance before pressing his hand to the glass door.

Before he could open it, another truck screamed sideways into the parking lot.

Rider cringed.

Shane Fetterlein slipped down out of the driver's seat and glared at the Hispanic men, muttering beneath his breath, something about *going back to Mexico.*

Praying the man wasn't out to pick a fight, Rider entered the store, hoping the ugliness would work itself out.

"Hi, Rider." Selena beamed at him as he entered the building.

He gave her brief nod, not wanting to think of *little Selena* as anything other than the foreman's daughter and hands-off. "Selena."

"What can I help you with today?" she asked, her smile bright, her enthusiasm ever-present.

Her level of cheerfulness almost irritated Rider. "I'm here for a cup of coffee," he said, his gaze returning to what might be trouble brewing outside.

Selena's glance followed his. Her smile slipped, and a frown dented her smooth brow. But when she faced him again, the smile was back. "How's work at your shop coming along today?"

Rider didn't want to admit he hadn't touched a

single vehicle that morning since he'd opened the letter. He shrugged. "It's going."

"I was out at the ranch yesterday." Selena rearranged the items on the counter in front of her as she spoke. "It's good to see your mother and father back from all of their travels."

"Yes, it is." Rider snagged a stick of beef jerky and a power drink from one of the coolers.

"I'm going with Lily to the Ugly Stick Saloon Friday night for the Annual Cowboy Bachelor Auction. Are you putting your name in the hat as one of the bachelors to be auctioned this year?"

"Hell—uh, no." He shivered at the thought of putting himself up on the stage at the Ugly Stick Saloon to be sold like a steer at a cattle auction.

Her smile twisted into a wry grin. "That's a shame. I'm sure you'd bring quite a big price for the children's charity."

He shook his head. "Sorry. Not my thing. Have you asked Chance?"

Selena's smile widened. "Oh, he's already signed up."

Figured. Chance liked living in the fast lane. He was a sponge for attention and loved the women. "Good. He'll represent the Graysons."

Selena sighed, her smile turning downward. "I would have bid on you, Rider, and saved you from all those hungry females."

He shot a glance at her. "You would have?"

"Of course." Her smile returned.

His brow descended. "I wouldn't want you to spend your hard-earned money on me."

She shrugged. "I've been saving, just in case."

"I've heard some of the guys at the auction go for a lot of money." Rider gave her a narrow-eyed stare. "What if someone outbid you?"

"Then I'd be disappointed. It's not often I get Rider Grayson alone for a few minutes of his time."

He stared at her, his groin tightening unexpectedly. Shifting uncomfortably, he stared across the racks of candy and chips. "And what would you do with that few minutes of time?" As soon as he asked the question, he wished he hadn't. A myriad of possibilities raced through his mind, none of them thoughts he should be having about her. Selena was the ranch foreman's daughter, and because of that, off-limits. He didn't live on the ranch anymore, but still…

A rosy blush filled Selena's cheeks. "Shoot, Rider. It's been a long time since I've gone horseback riding, or even walking along the creek on the ranch. Or even dancing at the Ugly Stick. I wouldn't take advantage of you. But it would be nice to spend a little time with you. You're like a brother to me." She flung a hand in the air. "It's not like I'm going to ask you to marry me or be the father of my children. I consider you *safe*. Not husband material. Because, the Lord knows, I don't need a husband right now."

When he should have felt relief, instead a stab of disappointment hit him square in the gut. Selena thought of him as a brother. Standing in the store, staring at the gorgeous, curvy figure of the foreman's grown-up daughter, Rider wasn't imagining anything brotherly about a date with Selena.

"Right." He cleared his throat and shifted his weight, hoping to relieve some of his body's reaction to the woman in front of him. "You know, all you have to do is ask, and I'll take you riding."

Her lips twisted, and she lowered her eyelids, staring down at the counter. "You're a busy man."

"Never too busy for *Little Selena.*"

She snorted. "I'm not so little anymore."

"I know." Rider tore his gaze away from her curvy figure and stared out the window. He stiffened. Shane stood toe to toe with Raul Jemenez, the leader of the Hispanic group, glaring down his nose at the man who stood a few inches shorter. He yelled something, and the Hispanic man pushed Shane.

"Oh no, you didn't, Raul Jemenez!" Selena muttered.

Before Rider knew what she was about, *Little Selena* vaulted the counter and ran out the door yelling, "Don't do it, Raul! Don't you dare start a fight." Her English quickly switched to rapid-fire Spanish.

Rider couldn't begin to keep up with the woman's movements, much less the translation. He'd meant to bone up on his Spanish skills. Now was too late. He ran out of the store after her.

SELENA CHARGED toward Raul and Shane, her fists at the ready. Why did men have to be such dumbasses? All that posturing and strutting only led to anger and fistfights.

Before Selena made it through the door, Shane swung with a left jab, catching Raul in the jaw. The man staggered backward a few steps, and then brought up his fists. He swung, his fist connecting with Shane's gut.

The redneck grunted, doubled over and plowed into Raul, driving him backward into his group of Hispanic cohorts and closer to the glass windows of the convenience store.

Great. Their fight might end up breaking the window. If the store closed for repairs, she'd lose out on several days' pay, and she wouldn't be able to make her rent. Selena pushed up her sleeves and advanced on the fighting men.

The two parted enough for Selena to get between them and plant a hand on each man's chest. "Stop fighting!" she commanded.

"Stay out of this, Selena," Raul said in Spanish.

"You're in America," Shane shouted. "Speak English."

Selena glared at Shane. "In America, we have the right to free speech."

"In English," Shane insisted.

"Nowhere in the constitution does it say, 'in English'." Selena shook her head. "But that's not the point. If you two are going to fight, take it somewhere else besides in front of the store window."

"We have the right to fight any damn where we want," Shane said.

"Not in front of this store, you don't," Selena said.

"Why don't you and your boyfriend go back to where you came from?" Shane said.

Anger burned low in Selena's belly. She knew Shane was nothing but an overgrown playground bully, but his words hurt. "And where do you think I came from, Shane Fetterlein?"

"Yeah, Fetterlein. Where do you think we came from?" Raul lifted his chin and glared at the big, white jerk.

"Mexico," Shane practically spat. "You and your kind need to go back, and take all your squalling brats with you." He shoved Selena's hand away from his chest and threw a punch at Raul.

Raul ducked.

The punch glanced off Selena's temple and sent her stumbling backward.

Anger burned so brightly, she couldn't think of anything but planting her own fist in Shane's nose. A growl rose up her throat and came out as a roar as she rushed toward Shane.

She didn't get two steps before strong arms wrapped around her waist and pulled her back against a solid wall of muscles. "Let go of me," she demanded, struggling to free herself from the bands of steel around her middle.

"Not until you promise you'll go back into the store and call 911," a familiar voice said into her ear.

She craned her neck around to see Rider staring down at her. She wriggled, trying to free herself from his grip. "Let me down. Those two are going to kill each other."

Meanwhile, Raul and Shane were well into trading punches.

"Make that call before the rest of their gangs join in." Rider set her on her feet and gave her a gentle shove toward the store. "Hurry."

She started toward the door and stopped when she realized Rider wasn't following her. "What are you going to do?"

"I needed a little distraction." He winked. "I'm going to stop this fight." He turned and dove in between Shane and Raul.

Within a second of butting in, Rider took a hit to his left cheek.

Selena's first instinct was to rush in and protect

Rider, but she wasn't big enough to stop three grown men from killing each other. Instead, she ran into the store, reached over the counter and grabbed the telephone.

The dispatcher answered on the first ring. "County sheriff emergency contact, what's your emergency?"

"Ava, it's Selena. We've got a fight going at the Gas-N-Go."

"Got a unit coming your way. Who's in it? Should I be jealous?"

Selena smiled. Ava was one of her classmates from high school. "Shane Fetterlein and Raul Jemenez got into it, and Rider Grayson is trying to stop it."

"I'd pay money to see that one," Ava said. "Is Rider going to be at the bachelor auction this Friday night?"

Selena strained to see what was going on outside the store. "No way. Gotta go, Ava. Can't see from where I am."

"Gotcha. See ya Friday."

Selena slammed the phone on the counter and ran back out in to the parking lot in time to see Rider wiping blood from his lip. Raul and Shane stood a few steps away, and a few steps apart, each bent over, breathing hard.

One of Shane's buddies took a step forward.

Rider pointed at the man. "Bobby Joe Crane, you

lift a fist to this fight, and I'll tell your mother. I used to mow her lawn for her when you were too small to reach the mower handle. Just think how disappointed she'd be to hear what her son's getting into trouble over."

Shane straightened. "Wouldn't be no trouble if these damned Mexicans would go back home."

"Their homes are here." Rider stared at the group of Hispanic men, ready to jump into the fight but hanging back because Rider was there. "How many of you were born in the United States?"

Every one of the men raised a hand.

Shane spat blood on the ground. "Then they need to learn to speak English."

"They have just as much of a right to speak Spanish as you have to wear blue jeans." Rider squared his shoulders. "You need to get over yourself, Shane. You grew up with Raul and Andres and Juan. They're residents of this country, this state and Hellfire. They're here to stay, and we should all be damned proud of such a rich and diverse heritage."

Selena's heart swelled with pride at Rider's defense of her people.

Shane snorted. "You're one to be talking." He jerked his head toward Selena. "You've employed wetbacks out at the ranch for decades. You rich ranchers are part of the problem. You like 'em so much, why haven't any of you married one?" The man sneered. "That's right. Because you're too good to marry beneath you."

Rider's fists bunched, and he plowed into Shane, knocking him onto his ass.

Shane sat on the ground, chuckling. "What's wrong, Grayson? Does the truth hurt?"

Before he could answer, a siren sounded behind Selena. She spun in time to dart out of the way of a sheriff's vehicle pulling into the parking lot. She was kind of sad the deputy had arrived before Rider answered the question.

Raul stepped forward and slipped his arm around Selena's waist. "Grayson hasn't married Selena, because she's my woman."

Rider's gaze met hers. Was that disappointment in his eyes? Whatever it was lasted a split second before being hooded beneath that enigmatic look all the Graysons were so good at displaying.

Selena shoved Raul's arm away. "I'm not your girl-friend. We broke up over a year ago."

"You broke up with me," Raul reminded her. "I didn't break up with you."

"So, that means it's not official?" Selena crossed her arms over her chest. "*You* have to be the one to say it? Is that so?"

Raul held up his hands. "I'm just saying, I haven't given up."

Selena shook her head. "You might as well move on. I'm not marrying you, or any other man, in this town. I'm going away for two years to school. I won't have time for anyone during that two years."

"Yeah, you say that now." Raul nodded toward Rider. "If Grayson asked you today, you'd change your tune."

Heat rose up her neck into her cheeks. "You're wrong. I had a little girl's crush on him. I'm all grown up now. I don't need the complication of a man in my life right now. I'm going to PA school." She pointed to Raul, and then to Rider. "No man is going to get in my way."

Deputy Nash Grayson stepped out of the sheriff's SUV. "What's going on here?"

"Nothing." Selena smiled at Nash. "The fight is over."

CHAPTER 2

RIDER GRINNED as Selena marched into the convenience store and back to work. The woman had spunk and didn't take crap from any man.

"You mind telling me why I received a call about a fight?" Nash addressed the men standing in the parking lot. "Anyone feel like spending the afternoon in jail? I'd be glad to take any volunteers. It's been a slow day."

Rider turned his grin on his brother. "You're a little slow. Had you been a few minutes earlier, I could have used your help."

Nash nodded toward Shane. "Fetterlein, you been pushing people around again?"

"They got no business in this country," Shane grumbled from his position on the ground where Rider had sent him.

"You're not going to win that argument." Nash

crossed his arms over his chest. "You might as well get over it and learn to get along." He reached out a hand to help the man to his feet.

Shane ignored it and rose on his own volition. He shot a glare at Rider. "Shouldn't have stuck your nose into something that wasn't your business."

"This town is my business," Rider said. "I live here, too."

"Yeah, well maybe you should go back to Dallas and your wife."

"Yeah, and leave our women to us," Raul added.

Nash stared from Raul to Shane and back to Rider. "Would someone like to let me know what's going on?"

"I don't know what Shane's talking about. I don't have a wife, and I live here in Hellfire." He turned to Raul. "And you. What the hell are you talking about?"

"I'm not stupid." Raul's lip curled back. "I see what's going on between you and my girl."

Rider shook his head. "Selena's not your girl. She said so herself. So, back off."

"Yeah, but you got eyes for her, and she's got 'em for you." Raul held up his hand. "Don't bother denying it. I can see it for myself." He walked up to Nash. "I got no trouble with your brother. We're just here to get gas for the truck and go back to work."

Nash nodded, his brow furrowing. "You let me know if you need help."

Raul glanced over his shoulder at Shane. "Yeah. I'll

help myself. Your kind sticks up for each other. So does ours." He gave Shane a hard look then walked away.

Shane jerked his head toward his gang of rednecks. "Let's go."

The parking lot cleared of the first truckload of angry men. Raul put fuel in his tank and left shortly afterward, leaving Nash and Rider standing there alone.

Nash clapped his hands together once and grinned. "Well, I'm glad I got to clear up that little fight. Sure broke the boredom of a day in the life of a deputy sheriff in Hellfire, Texas." Then his face sobered. "Perhaps you can tell me what the hell just happened here, and who gave you that shiner?"

Rider raised a hand to his eye. When he touched the skin across his cheekbone, he winced. "Not sure which one clocked me." He grinned. "But I got a few good ones in before it was all over."

Nash shook his head. "Please, tell me you didn't start the fight."

Rider looked at his brother as if he'd grown horns. "Seriously? You know me better than that. I went in to break it up."

"You look like you had too much fun for just trying to break up a fight."

Rider rubbed the backs of his knuckles. "I have to admit. I needed to let out a little aggression." He filled in his brother on how Shane had picked the fight with Raul, and how Selena had gotten in between them. "I would have let them work it out on their own, but when *Little Selena* took a hit, I couldn't let it go."

Nash chuckled. "*Little Selena.* You might not have noticed, but our little sidekick has grown up."

Rider nodded, his gaze going to the woman standing at the counter, holding a cup against her temple. "Yeah. When did that happen?"

Nash's gaze followed Rider's. "While you were up in Dallas, living the lifestyle of the rich and famous. Did you know she's about to graduate with her undergraduate degree in pre-med biology?"

"Already?" Rider dragged his gaze from Selena back to his brother. "When did that happen?"

"Over the past five years. She's been going to night school and driving into the city to take classes, while working a couple of jobs. I bet you also didn't know that she's been accepted in Physician Assistant school, starting next January." Nash raised his brows and met Rider's stare.

Rider shoved a hand through his hair and turned to look again at Selena. He had known she'd been applying, but he hadn't heard she'd been accepted. "Where have I been?"

"Gone for four years and checked out for another." Nash backhanded him in the gut. "You need to come *all the way* back to Hellfire, if you're going to make it your home."

His appreciation for the Hispanic spitfire grew. "All that, and she worked full time."

"Oh, and Mom and Dad want you at the dinner table tonight. Be there. Beckett's bringing Kinsey, and Phoebe's coming."

The thought of sitting at the family dinner table where his two brothers would be with their women, happily in love, made Rider want to throw something. "I've got work to do."

"You'll be there. Otherwise, Mom will be over with soup and her special stomach remedy to cure what ails ya." Nash chuckled at Rider's grimace. "Next time call sooner. I need something to kill the boredom. Everything's been pretty dead in town, lately."

"Sounds like the town is running smoothly."

"Which is a good thing, but I was looking forward to busting up a good-natured fight." Nash grinned. "Maybe there'll be one at the Ugly Stick Saloon tomorrow night. It's the Annual Cowboy Bachelor Auction. You gonna put yourself up for bid?"

"Hell, no," Rider said. "I'm barely single again."

"You're right. You might not be up to all that female adoration so soon." Nash frowned. "Actually, it might be just what the doctor ordered, after marriage to the ice queen." He pounded Rider on the back. "Give it some consideration. It's for a good cause."

"I know. For the children." Rider held up his hand. "Yeah. Yeah."

Nash laughed. "I see you've already been asked. Be ready for it, tonight. I think Mom's got your number."

All the more reason not to go to dinner that night.

"Forget it." Nash pointed at him. "You're coming." He spun on the heel of a uniform boot and headed for his SUV.

Damn Nash. If he hadn't seen him, he might not have gotten the invite and wouldn't have had to show up and sit with one big happy family. He didn't feel like being happy. He'd thought throwing a few punches would help make him cheerier, but that hadn't happened.

His gaze went to the woman in the store, the desire to enter and talk to this different person from the *Little Selena* he'd grown up with on the ranch nearly irresistible.

No. He couldn't go there. Besides, Selena had made it quite clear. She wasn't getting involved with any man. The woman was headed off to PA school in January.

Instead, Rider strode toward his motorcycle, mounted and drove back to his shop. Thoughts of his ex-wife were shoved completely to the back of his mind, replaced by a vision of a pair of rich brown eyes and long, dark, hairspray-free hair a man could sink his hands into.

SELENA SIGHED as Rider sped off on his Harley. Though she'd told Raul she didn't have time for a man in her life, she'd lied about her crush on Rider Grayson being strictly in the past. Her heart couldn't deny the attraction still existed and was stronger than ever. Something about Rider Grayson had captured a young girl's heart when she'd been too young to know better. She'd been heartbroken when he'd married the Dallas debutante. The fact he'd married the privileged woman only drove the wedge between them deeper, reminding her they didn't operate in the same circles.

She was the foreman's daughter. Her father was a first-generation Mexican immigrant, who'd paid his dues, earned his citizenship and established himself in this country. But he knew his place. He was the foreman, not family. The Graysons were the owners of a large ranch. The two classes of people did not mix. Her father had drilled into her head she was not to mingle with the boss's kids. She was not one of them. Her little girl's mind hadn't been able wrap itself around that fact, and she'd tagged along on many adventures with the Grayson boys and their sister, Lily.

When Rider had married Lydia Farnsworth of the Farnsworth Dynasty of Dallas, the elaborate wedding had been all over the news, like America's version of royalty. The wedding venue itself had cost over one hundred thousand dollars. The gown had been a whopping fifty thousand.

All Selena could think was that amount of money could have paid for her to attend Physician Assistant school several times over. Okay, and the wedding had also brought her childhood dream of marrying Rider Grayson to a sad end.

Now that he was back from Dallas, and freshly divorced, a spark of hope dared to fill her chest and swell. That spark had no business building. She had a job to do. Her job was to get her education and become the PA she was determined to be. Rider Grayson was still the man he was born to be, a member of the Grayson clan of ranch owners, who were in a different class from her and her family. She would not be distracted by him or the fact he was now an available bachelor.

But that didn't mean she shouldn't thank him for saving her from a busted lip or broken nose. Why she thought she could break up a fight between two hot-headed opponents was beyond her. Next time, she'd let the arrogant bastards beat each other senseless.

When her shift ended at noon, she spent the next few hours at the library, studying. Then she went home to the apartment she rented over Lola Engel's garage. Lola had given her a great deal on the place, allowing her to live there for practically nothing while she was still attending school.

In her little kitchen, she pulled out the ingredients for Mexican sugar cookies. She knew them to be among Rider's favorites when he was growing up. Her mother, the ranch's cook, had made them for him for every special occasion. He'd often been caught sneaking more when he'd thought no one was looking.

Selena smiled. Back then, she'd always hid a couple extra to give to him after he'd completed his chores in the barn. He'd always been happy to see her and the cookies.

The sound of footsteps on the stairs outside her door made Selena's ears perk and her heartbeat kick up a notch. Had her musings conjured the man himself?

"Selena, are you in there?" Lola Engel's voice sounded through the doorway. A moment later, a soft knock followed.

Selena set down her spatula and hurried to open the door.

Her landlady entered. "What's this I hear about a fight at the convenience store today?" Lola didn't wait for an introduction; she jumped right in.

Selena sighed. "Raul and Shane were having it out again in front of the store."

Lola shook her head. "I don't know what's wrong with those two boys, but they need to get a grip."

Selena nodded, placed a tray of cookies on a hot plate and moved them, one by one, from the tray to a plastic container. "I don't know why Shane can't get it through his thick skull that we all live here. We aren't going anywhere. It doesn't matter what race we are, we're all born and raised in Hellfire, Texas. We all need to learn to get along."

Lola picked up one of the cookies, sniffed it and smiled. "These are like the ones your mother makes, aren't they?"

Selena smiled. "To me, Mexican sugar cookies are comfort food. I make them when things get crazy. It helps to calm me down."

"I also heard you tried to break up the fight," Lola said, and then took a bite of a cookie.

Selena grimaced. "I don't know why I thought I could break up a fight between two big guys like that. But, I had to try. They're like two big bullies pushing each other around on the playground."

Lola laughed. "It's just like you to jump in the middle of it all. You have that fighting spirit in you, Selena. You always have a smile for everyone. And you don't like to see people get hurt."

Selena nodded. "I guess that's one of my faults."

Lola shook her head. "It's not one of your faults—it's one of your superpowers."

"I don't think I would call it a superpower." Selena shrugged. "But, whatever."

"Are you going to eat all of these cookies?" Lola raised her eyebrows at the two dozen cookies scattered across Selena's small kitchenette counter.

Selena gave her a crooked smile. "No, I thought I'd take them to Rider and thank him for pulling me out of the middle of the fight."

Lola's smile spread wider into a deep grin. "Do I detect a little attraction to the handsome Grayson brother?"

Selena shook her head. "No, I just want to thank him for helping me." Color rose in her cheeks, belying her words.

Lola's eyes narrowed. "Okay. Whatever you say." But her smile remained as she munched on the cookie.

Selena frowned. "It's not like we have anything in common."

Lola's smile turned into a frown. "What do you mean you don't have anything in common?"

Selena turned away to take another batch of cookies out of the oven. "Well, you know, he *is* one of the Grayson Ranch owners. My father's the foreman. You know."

Lola touched her shoulder. "So? You grew up around the Grayson brothers. You're like family to them."

"Careful. These are hot." Selena turned with the tray of cookies and set them on a hot plate on the counter. "Just because I grew up on the Grayson Ranch doesn't mean I'm one of the family." Although she had felt like one when she was growing up. She'd run alongside the brothers, as well as Lily. She'd played in the creek, ridden horses and played in the barn just like one of them.

Lola's frown deepened. "Horse feathers!" Her landlady grabbed a spatula and helped her take the cookies off the tray. "You are no better and no worse than one of the Graysons. We do not live in a caste system here. Just because you're Hispanic and he's white doesn't mean that you can't fall in love with a Grayson brother."

Selena's eyebrows rose into the hair drooping over her forehead. "What do you mean fall in love with a Grayson brother? I'm not in love with one of them. I'm not in love with Rider."

Lola's smile returned. "Right. I can see that. Go, take the cookies to Rider Grayson. I'm sure he will appreciate them. Most men do appreciate a woman who will take them cookies."

Heat rose in Selena's cheeks. She felt like the child with her hand caught in the cookie jar. Lola Engel could see right through her to things she didn't want anyone to know about herself.

Lola nodded took another cookie and headed for the door. "No worries, I'll leave you to your cooking. Say hello to Rider for me and, if his brother Chance is anywhere around, be sure to give him a wink and a kiss from Lola." The woman exited the apartment and ran down the stairs, laughing all the way.

Selena finished baking the cookies. When they were cool, she set some in a tin, pressed a top onto it and headed for the door. No matter what Lola said, she was just taking cookies as a thank you gift to Rider for pulling her out of the middle of a fistfight. Nothing more.

Selena exited her apartment, turned and locked the door behind her. Then she descended the stairs to the parking lot below and set out to walk the two blocks to Rider's garage. Several times along the way, she considered turning back and abandoning her attempt to thank Rider for helping her during the fight. Each time, her mother's voice sounded in her head, telling her it was the right thing to do.

Even with her mother's voice in her head, encouraging her to take the cookies as a thank you gift, Selena couldn't help but think visiting Rider was a really bad idea.

CHAPTER 3

RIDER DROPPED down on his back on the dolly and slid beneath the bright red antique Mustang he'd been working on all afternoon. With a wrench in hand, he loosened the drain plug on the oil pan and let the oil run into the bucket beside him. The familiar scents of oil, gasoline and the rubber of tires filled his senses, calming him, making him feel more at home and relaxed.

This was his element. Not the high rises of Dallas, nor the society-ridden galas of the swanky hotels. He'd gone to Texas A&M University to become a financial planner and help others decide where to put their money in the stock markets. He still did some of that on the side from his computer on the desk inside his office over the garage. Because of his smart investments and sales, it hadn't taken him long to refill his coffers after his divorce. He had a knack for betting on the right stocks.

His talents with the stock market made it possible for him to enjoy the physical skill of rebuilding cars and fixing engines, something hands-on where he could see the fruits of his labors immediately.

As he fitted a new oil filter in place on the 1967 Mustang, his thoughts drifted back to Selena at the convenience store and how she'd jumped into the middle of a fight between two heavy-set guys, twice her weight. The woman had more chutzpa than any of the debutantes he'd met in Dallas. She'd been that way even as a child growing up on the ranch. She went to bat for any underdog, determined to protect and defend.

He remembered her as the little girl who would do anything to follow him and his brothers and sister out to the fields. She wouldn't bother to throw a saddle on a horse, instead she'd mount bareback, hold onto the horse's mane and ride like the wind to catch up with them. Her jeans had been torn, her boots scuffed and her shirt dirty from playing as roughly as any of the boys. And when she rode, her dark hair flew back with the wind, tangled, but bright and shining in the sun.

Rider saw much of that little girl in the woman she'd become, only she had curves now, and her smile was brighter. Her eyes flashed when she was angry and sparkled when she smiled at anybody who entered her convenience store.

Selena and Raul had been an item at one point in time. Perhaps that was why she had jumped into the fray to break up the fight earlier. Had he misread Selena's intentions? Did she still have feelings for Raul?

A tug of disappointment settled in his gut. She deserved better. Raul worked construction, which wasn't a bad thing. But he lived in a rundown trailer and drank heavily.

Selena had her sights set on higher education and a better life for herself. Rider had no aspirations for dating the beautiful Hispanic girl he'd grown up with. She had never shown any interest in him other than that of a sister to a brother while growing up on the ranch. But after seeing her today, throwing herself into the middle of a fight, he couldn't help but think of all that passion and how it could be channeled in bed.

The thought of Selena in anyone else's bed made Rider's head jerk up, and he bumped it against the chassis of the car above him.

Footsteps sounded on the concrete near the entrance of the garage.

"I'll be with you in a moment." Rider tightened the drain plug on the oil pan and rolled out from beneath the car. His eyes widened. Standing before him, carrying a tin, stood the woman he'd just been thinking about. Heat filled his cheeks at the thought of Selena lying in a bed carrying a tin that smelled deliciously of her mother's Mexican sugar cookies.

"Selena, what are you doing here?" Rider frowned and raised his head too soon, not realizing that he hadn't quite cleared the frame of the car. He smacked his forehead against the metal and dropped his head back. Pain knifed through his forehead, and he groaned.

Selena went to her knees beside him and set the tin on the ground. "Rider, are you okay?"

Rider pressed a hand to his forehead. "I'm fine." His words came out a little sharper than he intended, more out of anger at himself than at being interrupted by Selena appearing in his garage.

Selena pressed her fingertips to his forehead, a frown denting her brow. "I'm sorry. I should have made my presence known."

Rider slid further from beneath the vehicle and sat up on the dolly. "No, that was my fault. I should have paid more attention to where I was."

Selena lifted the can and rose to her feet. "I brought you some of your favorite cookies."

Rider frowned. "What's the occasion?"

Selena shrugged "It's just a thank you for pulling me out of the fight earlier today."

"You don't have to thank me. Those guys would've hurt you. They were so set on bashing each other's faces in, they didn't even realize you were between them."

Selena grimaced. "I know. Those two just can't seem to get along."

"I don't know why they couldn't have taken it somewhere else other than the convenience store where you work."

"I'd just as soon they have their fight in front of the convenience store. That way I'm there to break it up." Selena raised her hand. "Even if I have to call the police, rather than jump in the middle." She grimaced. "I hate to think of them beating each other senseless and no one stopping them."

Rider shook his head. "You always think of others. You need to think about your own safety sometimes."

"Hellfire is my home," Selena said. "I just want everyone to get along."

Rider gave her a twisted grin. "Sometimes, you just have to accept that not everyone will get along."

Selena lifted her chin. "I'm not ready to accept that." She pushed the tin of cookies toward him. "Anyway, these are for you. Thank you for helping me out earlier."

Rider wiped the oil off his hands and accepted the tin. "Well, thank you for the cookies. I'd say they aren't necessary, but…" he sniffed drawing in a deep breath and letting it out, "these cookies smell so good I can't refuse."

Selena smiled. "They're just like my mother's. And I know how much you enjoy her sugar cookies."

Rider's smile spread across his face. "You always brought me an extra cookie after your mother baked them."

Selena shrugged. "I knew how much you liked them."

"Is that the only reason why you came by today?" Rider opened the tin and selected a cookie.

Selena glanced away, color filling her cheeks. "Of course."

"I was wondering…" Rider straightened to his full height.

Selena tipped her head back, staring up into his eyes. "Yes…?"

"I was wondering…" he paused to draw a deep breath, "are you and Raul a thing?"

Selena blinked several times, and a smile quirked the corners of her mouth. "Me and Raul?"

Rider lifted one shoulder. "You know… Are you two dating?"

Selena's grin spread across her face. "Not for a long time. Not for a year or so. Raul and I are on different paths."

"I just wondered if that was why you jumped into the middle of the fight." Rider shrugged nonchalantly although, inside, he relaxed at the news. "Not that it's any of my business."

"Why do you ask?" Selena tilted her head to the side.

"No reason. I just thought you two were so very different."

"We are. We want different things in life," Selena said.

"What do you want Selena?" Rider stared down into her eyes, noticing for the first time the flecks of gold in her brown eyes.

Selena stared up at him for a moment without speaking. "I want a better life for myself and my parents."

He blinked. "I didn't think your parents had such a bad life, working at the ranch."

Selena shook her head. "They don't have a bad life. But, one of these days, I would like to see them retire."

"And you think that improving your life will help them to retire sooner?" Rider said.

"No, I don't think it would help them to retire sooner. But I am their only daughter, and because of that, I know I'll be taking care of them when they get older." She gave him a tight smile. "I want to be in a position where I can care for them in comfort."

"There ya go again," Rider said. "Always taking care of others. That's what I like about you."

Selena stared up at him a moment longer. "Why did you leave Dallas?"

Rider turned away and placed the tin of cookies

on a shelf before answering. "Dallas wasn't for me. Hellfire is my home."

"You see? That's the same for me," Selena said. "Hellfire is my home as well. And I'd like to see the people who live here, live in peace."

Rider opened his mouth about to ask Selena if she would like to go out for a drink at the Ugly Stick Saloon, but before he could ask, a vehicle pulled up outside the open garage door, and he recognized the car as one of the sheriff's deputy's vehicles.

His brother Nash stepped out and looked over the top of the SUV. "Hey, Rider," Nash called out. "We'll see you at dinner tonight, won't we?"

Rider gave his brother a chin lift. "I'll be there."

Nash nodded. He tipped his hat, climbed back in his vehicle and drove away.

Selena glanced down at her hands, and then back up at Rider. "I guess I'd better get back to my studies."

"When do you start Physician Assistant school?" Rider asked.

Selena glanced up, a sparkle in her eyes. "I was accepted into the program beginning in January. I can't believe I got in my first try."

"It's your determination and dedication to getting the job done that got you in," Rider said.

"My determination and half a dozen letters of recommendation from some pretty prominent people that somebody helped me acquire." Her brows rose. "Thank you for getting those for me from the doctors in Dallas. I appreciate it."

"I knew how hard you had worked in your undergraduate degree. I did what I could to make sure you got the opportunity to continue your education." Rider lifted a shoulder. "I'm happy to hear the recommendations helped you get in. You deserved it."

Selena touched his arm. "Thank you for today and for the recommendations. You don't know how much they meant to me." She leaned up on her toes and pressed a kiss to his cheek. Then she turned and ran from the garage.

Rider stood for a moment, watching her disappearing figure. He raised his hand to where her lips had touched his cheek and felt a tingle he hadn't felt in a long time. Now was not a good time to be thinking these kinds of thoughts about a girl who'd been like a sister growing up. But Rider couldn't stop those thoughts nor the tug in his groin at her curvy shape and the fullness of her lips.

He finished working on the Mustang, pouring oil back into the oil pan and cleaning up the mess he'd made. When he finished, he glanced at the clock. It was almost five-thirty, and his mother liked to serve dinner promptly at six. If he was going to make it there on time, he'd have to hurry. He closed up the shop, ran upstairs to his apartment above the garage and jumped into the shower.

A few minutes later, he was clean, wearing fresh

jeans and a button-up white shirt and cowboy boots. He raced down the stairs, hopped on his Harley and zoomed out of town to the ranch where he'd grown up. He wondered if Selena would be visiting her parents that evening. If so, he might take her for a walk at sunset. Just to remind himself of old times. Like a brother enjoying the sunset with a sister. Like hell!

"MAMA, I don't know why you need me to help you with dinner tonight. You're perfectly capable of feeding an army, alone, and with one hand tied behind your back. I had a lot of studying to do and needed that time to go over my books and make notes." Selena helped ladle BBQ sauce over the ribs and place them on a platter to be served at the dining table.

"Is it a sin to want my daughter to help me prepare the meal for my employers for this special occasion? The entire family is here tonight. I just wanted to make sure the dinner was perfect." Her mother hugged her. "I knew I could count on you."

Selena sighed. "You know you can always count on me, Mama."

Her mother smiled. "I know, *mi hija*."

Selena lifted the tray of BBQ ribs and carried it through the kitchen and out into the formal dining room of the ranch house. She set the platter in the middle of the table and returned to the kitchen for the bowl of potato salad.

Selena's father entered through the back door.

Her mother turned to him. "Wash your hands, Papa."

Without hesitation, her father walked to the sink, washed his hands and then turned to her mother.

She placed a platter of bread rolls in his hands. "Take these to the table, *por favor*."

Selena grinned. Her father followed orders as well as he gave them. He knew his place, and Mama was always right. Selena hefted the huge bowl of potato salad in her arms and carried it out to the dining room. Already, the Grayson family, gathered in the living room, was heading toward the dining room.

Nash Grayson led the way, sniffing as he came. "Something smells wonderful." Nash patted his belly.

Phoebe Sinclair followed Nash into the dining room. "Wow, that really does smell good."

Big John Grayson, father of the Grayson brothers, entered the room with his wife Ann on his arm. "Are those Margarita's famous pork ribs I smell?"

Selena nodded and placed the potato salad on the table. "Mama worked hard on those ribs. They're so tender they're falling off the bone."

Ann Grayson smiled at Selena. "I hope you and your family will consider joining us for dinner tonight."

Selena shot a glance at her father carrying in the rolls.

Her father shook his head. "We have already had dinner." He shot a glance towards Selena, his eyes narrowing slightly.

Selena knew her father's statement was a lie. He always said the same thing when asked to join the family at the dinner table. Her chest tightened. Just once she would have liked to join the Grayson family at the dinner table. She had always felt like one of them. Until it came to dinner time. Beckett Grayson entered with his fiancée Kinsey Phillips, a young lady Selena was very aware of, having grown up riding horses alongside her as well as the Grayson family.

"That's right. How come Pedro and Margarita have always finished eating when we sit down for our own meal?" Beckett asked.

Selena's father dipped his head. "We were hungry?" He smiled and backed out of the room into the kitchen. Selena refused to meet Rider's gaze as he entered the dining room. She set the potato salad on the table and turned to leave. By the time Selena, Margarita and Pedro had ferried all the food out to the table, the entire Grayson family had arrived, including Chance, who skidded in just as the clock struck six o'clock.

Ann Grayson glanced at the old grandfather clock and raised her brows. "Nice of you to join us, Chance."

Chance grinned. "Always good to have dinner with the fam." He took his seat at the side of the table. Big John Grayson sat at one end of the table, and his wife Ann sat at the other end. Nash and Beckett sat on one side of the table with their fiancées, Phoebe and Kinsey. Rider and Chance sat on the other side. Ann Grayson said grace while all bowed their heads.

Selena watched from the kitchen, checking the table over one more time to make sure they had brought out everything the family would need for their dinner. When she was certain they had everything, she let the door close between the kitchen and the dining room. This was how it had always been since she could remember. The Grayson family sat at the formal dining room table, while the Sanchez family carried their plates to the table in the kitchen and sat and ate in silence. A long time ago, her father had explained, "We are the servants in this household. The Grayson family sits at the formal dining table. We do not."

When Selena turned away from the dining room door, her mother met her with a plate full of the delicious ribs she'd cooked. "Please, sit down. Enjoy."

Selena took the plate and sat in the seat she had always sat in as a child to the left side of her father. Her mother took a seat on the right side of her father. They bent their heads, said grace, and then lifted their forks and began to eat. A moment later, the kitchen door swung open, and Rider entered carrying his plate.

Selena jumped to her feet. "Is there something wrong with the food?"

Rider shook his head, walked to the table and sat in the chair beside Selena's. "I hope you don't mind if I join you."

Selena stood for a moment her mouth slightly agape. "Is there something wrong with the dinner table?"

Rider shook his head. "Nope." He lifted his fork, dug into the tender flesh of the pork ribs and jammed a bite into his mouth. "Mmmmmm. Mrs. Sanchez, these are the best ribs ever."

Margarita Sanchez grinned. "*Gracias*, Rider."

A moment later, Chance Grayson entered the kitchen carrying his plate. Without a word, he took the seat next to Rider and dug into his food.

Lily Grayson entered next, a smile spreading across her face. She sat next to Margarita Sanchez without saying a word. One by one, the entire Grayson family entered the room carrying their plates. Last to enter was Big John Grayson. He too held his plate in his hand, his eyebrows raised. "I don't know why we eat in that big ol' dining room, when the table in the kitchen is plenty big enough for all of us." He carried his plate to one of the seats on the side of the giant table that had served many a meal to ranch hands and owners alike. "I see you were hungry enough for seconds." He nodded toward the Sanchezes' full plates.

Selena's father nodded. "Yes, sir."

Before long, conversation flowed, laughter rang out and the room filled with warmth and love.

Ann Grayson broke through the laughter with a statement, drawing attention to herself, "Chance, I understand you've volunteered to be a bachelor at the Annual Cowboy Auction at the Ugly Stick Saloon." She turned to face Rider. "Rider? What about you?"

All gazes fixed on Rider.

Rider's cheeks reddened "I didn't plan on going to the cowboy auction."

His mother tilted her head and narrowed her eyes. "It's for a good cause," she said. "Why not volunteer?"

"Ha!" Lily laughed. "He's afraid of the women."

Rider stiffened. "I'm not afraid of the women."

Chance clapped him on the back. "You should be." He chuckled. "Last year, they got into a cat fight over one of the cowboys."

"They wouldn't fight over me." Rider shook his head. "Besides, no one asked me to volunteer."

Lily leaned forward. "Really? That can be reme- died." She grinned. "I'm on the nominating committee."

Selena grinned at the look on Rider's face. He held up both hands as if in surrender. "I'm sure you have plenty of cowboys who've already volunteered for the auction. You don't need me."

Lily shook her head. "We can always use good lookin' cowboys. You're not half bad, even if I am your sister. That's it... You're on for tomorrow night."

Selena ducked her head, hiding her smile.

"I can't believe I just got suckered into being a part of the cowboy auction." Rider groaned. "It's nothing but a meat market, and all the men are sides of beef."

Chance clapped him on the back. "It'll be fun. Hopefully, a young cute thing will bid on you."

"More like Mrs. Cleyburne will bid high enough to win me." Rider grimaced. "I can't imagine a date with Mrs. Cleyburne."

Chance, Nash, and Beckett all laughed.

When dinner was over, Selena gathered plates from the table and carried them to the sink.

"Let me help," said Rider's deep familiar voice behind her.

"I can get this," Selena said.

"I'll wash. You can dry." Rider lifted a dry dish towel and handed it to her. He filled the sink with warm soapy water and, one by one, washed the dishes.

Selena's mother finished clearing the table and storing the food in containers in the refrigerator.

When she was finished, she came to the sink. "I can take over now," she said.

Selena shook her head. "No, Mama. You go rest. You've worked hard. I can take care of the rest of these dishes."

"At least, let me take care of washing the dishes so that Rider can go enjoy his family." Mrs. Sanchez tried to take the wash rag from Rider's hands, but he blocked her with his body.

"I really can wash a dish or two," said Rider. "I took care of my own dishes when I lived in Dallas, and I'm sure I could do it again."

Selena exchanged glances with her mother and shrugged. "If he wants to do dishes, let him."

Rider chuckled. "Yes, please. Let me."

Mrs. Sanchez wiped the table and hung the wash rag in the laundry room. She walked back through the kitchen, her gaze scanning the countertops for any other dishes to clean. "Well, then I guess I'll leave you two to it."

Everyone else had gone out of the kitchen into the living room, leaving Rider and Selena at the sink washing dishes. The silence stretched between them as Rider washed and Selena dried and put the dishes away. "You know you don't have to do the cowboy auction," Selena said. "I'm sure you can back out and still save face."

"I don't really think I have a choice," Rider said.

"When Lily gets something in her mind, she doesn't let go."

Selena chuckled. "Lily does have a strong will. It will take her far in life."

"I feel sorry for the guy she falls in love with." Rider grinned. "I hope he has the balls to stand up to her when he needs to."

"You know, you could just donate the money and skip the auction altogether." Selena set another plate in the cabinet and turned to face him.

Rider shrugged. "I could, but then Lily wouldn't get a kick out of seeing me on stage, stripping my shirt off for the ladies." Rider grimaced. "I really don't look forward to doing that."

"You could spike the audience with someone who has your donation in hand and let her bid on you and win you, and that way you know who you're getting, and you don't have to go on a date with her since you're paying."

Rider tipped his head to the side and stared down at Selena. "You know, that's not a bad idea." He didn't mention that he'd had a similar conversation with Selena.

"Do you have a lady in mind?"

Rider emptied the dishwater from the sink and dried his hands. "Well, it can't be a family member, or the audience would know what was going on."

"You could ask my landlady Lola Engel," Selena

offered. Before she finished talking, Rider was shaking his head.

"No. From what I understand, she'll be bidding on Chance. She's had a thing for him for months now. She'll bid every dollar she has to go out on a date with my brother."

Selena grinned. "I guess she has been pretty blatant about her attraction to Chance. I hear she stages some pretty elaborate emergencies to get the fire department to come out on his shift."

Rider nodded. "I don't know what she sees in him. He's got to be at least ten years younger than she is."

"It might just be that the heart wants what the heart wants." Selena smiled. "Apparently Lola's heart wants Chance." She dried the last plate, set it in the cabinet and hung the towel across the rail on the stove. "Well, I guess I'd better get back to town."

"Can't you stay a few more minutes? If I remember correctly, there might be a meteor shower this evening," Rider said. "I have a couple of lounge chairs out on the porch if you care to join me. We can drag them out into the yard and see if we can spot any of the shooting stars."

Selena nodded. "I remember lying out under the stars at night during the meteor showers. One night, we counted thirty-seven altogether. That was a pretty magical night." Selena recalled lying there in the darkness, just her and Rider. His brothers and sister had all given up too early and had gone back into the house. But she'd stayed with Rider to watch the meteor shower as it lit up the sky.

"That was a pretty impressive night, wasn't it?" Rider led the way to the back door and held it for Selena as she walked through. Her shoulder brushed against his chest, sending a tingle of awareness across her skin and down her spine.

She hurried through and out onto the deck.

Rider grabbed the two folding lounge chairs and carried them out into the yard.

Selena hesitated. When they were kids, lying in the dark on the ground beside each other, it had been as natural as breathing. Now was a little different. Why was it different now? She studied the man as he straightened and waved a hand toward one of the lounge chairs he'd prepared. He'd grown into a very handsome, broad-shouldered man, with twinkling eyes and a thick head of hair. She could not deny the attraction she felt toward Rider Grayson. She'd always had a thing for him. And she'd always known she could never act on it. Especially not now, when she was starting Physician Assistant school in January. She had to retain her focus on her studies and be completely immersed in her schoolwork once classes started. She wouldn't have time for a relationship. And she certainly couldn't have a relationship with a Grayson brother.

"What's wrong?" Rider stared down at her in the starlight.

Selena shrugged. "Nothing. I'm just thinking I should be studying, instead of lying in the darkness staring up at stars."

"You're very dedicated to your work, and I admire that about you. But sometimes, you really do need to stare up at the stars. They make you realize what's really important."

Selena nodded. "You're right. It grounds you in reality and makes you realize you're not the center of the universe, although sometimes it feels like it."

"I'll go first," Rider said. He stretched out on a lounge chair, tucked his hands beneath his head, and stared up at the stars. "Look, there's one now."

Selena dropped down to the lounger and laid on her back, her attention on the sky above her, though she was fully aware of the man lying beside her. A flash across the sky caught her attention. "There's another," Selena said excitedly.

"And another," Rider said, pointing at the sky. As they both lowered their arms to the lounge, their fingers touched and entwined, and the next thing Selena knew, they were holding hands in the dark, staring up at the sky.

This was not how she'd planned for this night going. In fact, it was much better than what she'd envisioned. Unfortunately, she couldn't allow herself to enjoy it too much. Nothing between her and Rider could ever be more than just friends. They worlds apart in their dreams and aspirations, as well as in their heritage. Rider had returned home to Hell-fire to stay. She'd be leaving in January for two years. Who knew what would happen in that time? Rider could find a woman to love, get married and have a child in just two years. Meanwhile, Selena would be nose-deep in her books learning how to be a Physician Assistant with no time to spare for a relationship.

For that moment, however, she chose to ignore what the future might hold. Her hand in his was all that mattered. His fingers closed around hers, big, strong and warm.

"You know, I've been thinking about your suggestion," Rider said.

"What suggestion?" Selena asked.

"The one about having someone bid on me with *my* donation." He turned toward her. "Would you do that for me?"

Selena's heartbeat ratcheted up. When he looked at her like that, she'd do anything for him. But she couldn't tell him that. "You want me to bid on you at the cowboy auction tomorrow night?"

"Yes. You're the only one I can trust."

"How much are you willing to bid?"

"As much as it takes to keep anyone else from winning the bid," he said.

"That could go pretty high." Selena's hand squeezed his. "Are you sure?"

"I'm sure. The thought of having a date with Mrs.

Cleyburne gives me the willies." He chuckled. "Whereas, a date with you would be a lot more palatable."

"If I'm using your money to bid on you, you wouldn't have to take me out on the date," Selena reminded him.

"I wouldn't want anyone to think I had bid on myself," Rider said.

"So, we'd go on a fake date to calm any gossip." Selena nodded. "I'm in."

"Great." Rider laid back staring up at the stars. He retained his hold on her hand, squeezing slightly, the warmth spreading from her fingers all the way into her arm and low into her belly.

"You know, I couldn't see the stars in the sky when I was in Dallas," Rider said.

"That's sad," Selena said.

"They say everything is bigger in Texas. In Dallas, there's plenty of lights, glitz and glamour. But you don't have the big sky filled with stars. You don't see the meteor showers at night. You can't smell the fresh cut hay or hear the chirp of the cicadas. All you hear is the honking of horns, the sirens blaring and the noise of the city."

"I'll miss Hellfire, while I'm gone," Selena said.

Rider's fingers tightened around hers. "I'll miss you when you're gone."

The door opened to the house, and footsteps

sounded on the deck. "I thought they were out here." Nash's voice could be heard.

"I saw them come out earlier," Phoebe's responded in the darkness.

"Rider, you out there?" Nash called out.

Rider hesitated before answering, "I'm out here. Tonight's the meteor shower."

"Well, when you're done watching the meteor shower, we're all having ice cream and cake inside, if you'd like to join us," Nash said.

The door opened again and closed, and silence surrounded Rider and Selena.

"I guess that's our cue," Selena said.

"If you want it to be," Rider said.

She didn't want it to be the cue. She'd rather stay there the entire night holding Rider's hand and watching the meteor shower. But, she had studies to get on with. She had a test coming up in a couple of days that she needed to pour her heart into in order to make a good grade.

"I don't know about you, but ice cream sounds good." Selena rose from the lounge chair, pulling him up with their joined hands.

Rider stood beside her in the darkness. "When did you grow up, Selena?"

"While you were playing the stock markets in Dallas," Selena said, still holding his hand.

"I don't know how I missed it." Rider lifted her

hand and pressed his lips to her knuckles. "You're still the same ol' Selena. But, better."

"I'm still the same old Selena." She gave a hint of a smile.

"I know you're going to be busy with school for the next couple of years. When you do get ready for a relationship, don't settle for anything less than the best. You deserve it. Life is too short to settle for second best."

"I'll remember that."

Rider offered his arm.

Selena slipped her hand through the crook of his elbow and let him lead her back up the stairs into the house. After a small scoop of ice cream and a bite of cake, Selena made her excuses and slipped away into the night, driving back to her little apartment over the garage at Lola Engel's house.

Her heart squeezed tightly in her chest as she slipped into her nightgown and into her bed. She knew what she had to do, and that all her focus should be on her education. But holding Rider's hand that evening had opened her up again to the heartache of loving a man who could never love her in return. To him, she was like a sister. To her, he was the love she'd always dreamed of.

CHAPTER 4

RIDER PACED behind the curtain of the stage at Ugly Stick Saloon. The Annual Cowboy Auction was in full swing, and he'd been suckered into being one of the cowboys up for auction.

"What's wrong, bro?" Chance backhanded him in the gut. "All you gotta do is strut your stuff out there, maybe take off your shirt, and all the ladies will go wild."

Rider rolled his eyes. "That's what I'm afraid of. I don't want the women to go wild. I just want this to be over—with my shirt on."

Chance chuckled. "In order to bring in the best money for charity, you have to take off your shirt. The ladies love it. And if I'm not mistaken, you might still have some muscles there to show off." He poked a finger at Rider's shoulder.

"I don't care what the ladies will love," Rider said.

"All I promised was to show up. I did *not* promise to take off my shirt."

"You guys ready?" Lily walked through the array of men behind the stage. At her side was Audrey Anderson, the owner of the Ugly Stick Saloon.

"Men, I want to thank you all for taking the time and donating your services for the Annual Cowboy Auction. We raise more money for the children at this auction than any other organization in the tri-county area." Audrey Anderson grinned widely. "The kids deserve it, and don't worry, we'll keep it clean."

Lily grinned at Chance and Rider. "Don't look so glum Rider."

"I don't know how you got me into this." Rider shook his head.

"Don't be such a baby," Chance said. "And just to make you feel better, I'll go first," Chance said.

Audrey shook her head. "I have a specific lineup with bios for each of you. I will introduce you one at a time. The good news is, Chance goes before Rider. So, you will have your opportunity to go first."

"Y'all ready to raise some money?" Lily yelled over the noise coming from the other side of the curtain.

Chance yelled *Yes!* along with the other guys.

Rider shook his head.

"Then let's do it," Audrey Anderson said.

One by one, she introduced the men. And one by one they strutted out on the stage to the hooting and hollering of a couple hundred women filling the Ugly Stick Saloon. The first guy sold for a whopping seven hundred dollars. Rider was appalled, imagining the draining of his bank account as the different men went for different pledges. He'd given Selena the go ahead to bid as high as she needed to when the auction pulled him forward. The second guy bid out at just short of a thousand dollars, nine hundred and ninety dollars. "Holy shit," Rider said.

Chance chuckled. "Last year we had one guy go for over five thousand dollars."

"You're kidding me, right?"

"Nope, last year he went for over five thousand dollars. A woman from Dallas had come in and bid on him. She was some high-powered executive who needed a date. Anyway, she was willing to pay."

Lily poked her head backstage and said, "You're up, Chance."

"Here goes nothing," Chance said, and stepped through the curtain, his hands on the hem of his shirt. As soon as he stepped through, he yanked the shirt up over his head. A roar from the crowd made him dance around, grinding his hips.

Rider watched through the curtains, appalled at his brother's actions. There was no way in hell he was getting out there strutting his stuff and grinding his hips like his brother Chance. The best he would do was walk out on stage with his shirt on and stand there while they bid on him. As he watched, the bidding began. Starting at five hundred dollars. Holy hell, five hundred dollars was the starting point? That was insane.

The bidding jumped from five hundred to one thousand dollars. Within minutes it had gone to two-thousand dollars. By the time the bidding stopped, Chance had exceeded the five-thousand-dollar mark from last year at five thousand five hundred dollars.

Rider almost laughed out loud at the disgruntled look on Lola Engel's face, and the smile of glee on Mrs. Cleyburne's face. She'd won the bid. Hopefully, Mrs. Cleyburne had spent all her money on Chance and wouldn't have any left to bid on Rider.

"Rider, you're up," Lily said.

Chance danced back behind stage to the cheers of the crowd. He turned and gave Rider a shove, pushing him through the curtain out onto the stage in front of what appeared to be a million women all waving money toward him like he was a dancer at a Chippendale's show.

Bump and grind music played, and Rider searched the crowd for Selena. For one frightening moment, he couldn't find her and thought perhaps she'd decided not to come after all. Then his gaze met hers, and a sigh of relief filled his chest.

Once again, the bidding began at five hundred dollars. The first bid came from Lola Engel.

"Move around the stage," Lily urged from the sidelines.

Rider walked around the stage, feeling awkward.

"Take it off," a woman called out.

More women joined the chant, "Take it off! Take it off! Take it off!"

The bidding jumped to a thousand dollars.

Rider shot a quick glance at Selena. She grimaced and shrugged. He gave her a slight nod, encouraging her to continue bidding.

"Take it off," the crowd of women chanted. "Take it off!"

"Come on, baby." Lola Engel waved a wad of hundred-dollar bills above the crowd. "I've got two thousand dollars burning a hole in my pocket. Take off the shirt."

Rider shot a desperate glance towards Selena. She grimaced and raised her hand. "Two thousand and one hundred dollars," she cried above the crowd's noise.

Lola looked toward where she stood and frowned. "Two thousand and two hundred," Lola said.

Selena upped her bid, "Two thousand three hundred."

Another woman cried out, "Twenty-five hundred dollars!"

Lola waved her money in the air again. "Three thousand dollars. He's not Chance, but he's a Grayson brother, and by golly worth every penny."

Selena gave Rider a desperate glance. "Three thousand one hundred dollars," she yelled.

"Four thousand dollars," a woman yelled from the back of the room.

Rider tried to see who was calling out the bid, but he couldn't find the woman.

"Four thousand one hundred dollars," Selena cried out, her voice shaking.

"Lordy, girl." Lola laughed. "I'm gonna have to raise your rent, if you have that kind of money."

Rider couldn't believe how high the bidding had gone. He had the money in the bank, but holy hell, four thousand one hundred dollars?

From the back of the room, a woman yelled, "Five thousand dollars."

Selena looked to Rider.

He gave her a slight nod.

"Five thousand one hundred dollars!"

"Six thousand dollars," the woman cried from the back of the room.

Rider strained to see who was talking but couldn't find the source of the bid.

Selena cried out, "Seven thousand dollars!"

Rider held his breath, waiting. Seven thousand dollars was a lot of money. Granted, he could count it off on his taxes as a charitable contribution. But seven thousand dollars? To buy himself? It was insanity.

Still he held his breath and waited. The woman at

the back of the room remained silent. "Going, going, gone!" Audrey Anderson pounded the gavel against the podium. "Sold! To this young lady for seven thousand dollars. Congratulations on winning your cowboy for a date."

"Hey, he didn't take off his shirt," a woman yelled.

More women yelled, "No, he didn't take off his shirt. Take it off! Take it off!"

Before he could step down from the dais, a couple of women stormed the stage, grabbed his shirt, and ripped it off his body. If a man had done that to him, he would have decked him. But these were women, and his momma had taught him never to throw a punch at a woman. But oh, he was tempted.

Selena climbed up on stage and blocked more women from attacking him. "Back off," she yelled. "I won him fair and square."

Rider grinned and slipped his arm around Selena's waist. "That's right. She won the bid. I'm hers for the night."

Selena smiled up at him and whispered beneath her breath. "I hope I did okay."

He leaned down. "You sure did. Thank God."

Selena grimaced. "That was a lot of money."

"It's okay. I can afford it," Rider said.

"Let's sign the check and get out of here." Selena slipped her hand into his, and together they waded through the crowd to the table to pay, and then to the exit.

Outside the door, Rider sucked in a deep breath and let go of it. "Holy crap, that is more insanity than any man should have to suffer."

Selena giggled, and then her giggle turned into a laugh, and before long she was holding her sides laughing as hard as she could. "You should have seen your face when they yelled *take it off*." She laughed again.

"You weren't the one being mauled by a thousand horny women."

Selena tried but couldn't wipe the smile from her face as she looked up into his eyes. "Well, you did volunteer."

"Volunteer? I was pushed into this by Lily and Chance." He snorted. "So much for family looking out for each other. Never again." Rider glanced at Selena. "How did you get here tonight?"

She smiled. "I drove myself."

Rider glanced around the parking lot. "I rode with Chance. I don't suppose you have time to give me a ride home?"

"I guess since I won the bid, it would be nice of me to give you a ride home. All the money you brought in for the charity was a tremendous amount. The children will be happy." She nodded toward a vehicle sitting on the far side of the parking lot. "I'm parked under the light, way over there. Come on, let's get you home and into a shirt."

"That was one of my best shirts," he groused.

"All for a good cause," she reminded him.

As they approached her car, a figure detached itself from leaning against it.

"I HEAR you just dropped seven Gs on this *gringo*." Raul pushed away from the car and advanced toward Selena and Rider.

Great. Just when the evening had gone so well, Raul had to come along and spoil it. Selena crossed her arms over her chest. "What I spend my money on is none of your business, Raul."

"Is this why you dumped me?" Raul pointed at Rider. "For this *gringo?*"

"I didn't dump you because of Rider." Selena shook her head. "We didn't have anything in common, Raul. And I didn't appreciate you bossing me around. I'm my own person. I have my own idea of where I'm going in life. And it has nothing to do with you."

"He is a Grayson, Selena." Raul jerked his hand toward Rider. "Graysons don't marry Sanchezes."

"Just what's that supposed to mean?" Rider asked. "Are you saying the Graysons are better than the Sanchezes?"

Raul tipped his chin up. "It's true. The Graysons *think* they're better than anybody else in the county."

Rider shook his head. "That's not true. I don't think of myself as any better than Selena or any member of her family. So, they work for the Graysons. Everybody has jobs. The Graysons work the land, sell the cattle to keep in business. The Sanchezes work for the Graysons. We couldn't do what we do without their help."

Selena didn't jump into the argument. Her father had drilled into her head that the Sanchezes worked for the Graysons. They did not comingle or get silly ideas in their heads about marrying into the Grayson family.

Raul jerked his head toward Selena. "You think by going to school and becoming a Physician Assistant you'll become an equal to the Graysons. You're wrong," he said. "They'll never accept you as one of their own. You're Hispanic. You're not white. You will never fit in with the Graysons."

Rider took a step forward. "You don't know what you're talking about, Raul." Rider's hands bunched into fists.

Raul took another step toward Rider, his own fists coming up in front of him.

Selena stepped between them. "Raul, I don't know what you're talking about. It's not like I'm going after one of the Graysons. I have school ahead of me. I don't have time to be chasing after anyone. I am on a one-track path to get my education and become a PA. I want to help people who need my help. That does not include marrying a Grayson or marrying you, Raul. I have my own path, and I intend to follow it."

Raul snorted. "Yeah, well, seven grand is a lot of money that could've helped you toward your education."

"That seven thousand dollars is going toward a good cause. And where I got that seven thousand dollars is absolutely none of your business, Raul."

Raul sneered. "Yeah, well, seven thousand dollars is a lot of money to pay for a date with a man you've been panting after since you knew the difference between boys and girls."

Rider stepped forward. "Apologize to the woman," he demanded.

Raul sneered. "I'm not gonna apologize for stating the truth." He tipped his head toward Selena. "She's been panting after you all her life. Even when we were dating, all she could think about was you."

Heat filled Selena's cheeks. She was glad for the darkness so that Rider couldn't see her blushing. "None of it matters, Raul. The seven thousand dollars wasn't mine. I don't even plan on going on a date with this cowboy. I bid in the auction as a favor to a friend. Not that it's any of your business."

She stepped back and waved toward the two men. "If you guys want to bash each other's heads in, go for it. I'm not going to stop you." She pulled her keys out, stuck them into the lock on her car and twisted.

Rider stared at Raul, his eyes narrowed. "Leave Selena alone. Apparently, she doesn't want anything to do with you."

Raul gave him an answering glare. "You should have stayed in Dallas with your own kind. Selena isn't the one for you. If you hurt her, I'll kill you."

Selena gasped. "Raul Jemenez, you have no right to be threatening anyone. I can defend myself when I need to. I don't need you or anyone else sticking up for me. I can take care of myself." She slipped into the driver's seat and rolled down the window. "Rider, if you're hitching a ride with me, you'd better come now."

Rider stared at Raul a moment longer. "I'm going to let your threats slide this time," he said. "Because I truly believe you have Selena's best interests at heart, even though you're going about it all wrong." He backed a step, turned, rounded the back of the car and climbed into the passenger seat.

Selena backed out of the parking space, careful to avoid hitting Raul. She pulled out onto the road and hit the accelerator a little harder than she intended. But the anger inside made her push even harder. Selena sped toward Hellfire, still so angry her hands shook on the steering wheel.

"I'm sorry Raul was such a pain tonight." Rider's voice cut through the silence.

Selena didn't respond. So many thoughts were racing through her head, she wasn't capable of expressing any words. She didn't know who she was angrier with...herself or Raul.

On the one hand, everything Raul had said was

true. She didn't belong in Rider Grayson's world, and a Grayson would never marry a Sanchez. She was angry at Raul for pointing it out.

But she was angry at herself for harboring those little dreams stuck in the back of her mind. Dreams of her walking down the aisle toward Rider Grayson were just ludicrous. Yes, it was the twenty-first century, and yes, racism was supposed to have be a thing of the past. But with the current political climate, racism had gotten worse. She'd even been threatened by some of the more hardcore rednecks in Hellfire, telling her to go back to Mexico where she belonged, just the day before. The thing was, she didn't belong in Mexico. She'd been born and raised there in Texas.

Texas was her home. Having all the Graysons sitting around the kitchen table with the Sanchez family didn't change any of that, as much as she would have liked it. All these thoughts were spinning around in her head when she pulled to a stop in front of Rider's garage.

The headlights hit the walls of the building, exposing huge swaths of painted graffiti, with the message, *Go back to Dallas.*

Selena gasped.

Rider swore beneath his breath and jerked open his door. He jumped out and hurried toward the front of the building.

Selena, moving a little slower, exited the vehicle

and walked up to stand beside Rider. The letters were printed in bold red spray paint across windows, overhead garage doors, and on the building's siding.

"What the hell?" Selena said. "Who would have done this to you?"

Rider shook his head. "I don't know."

Selena pulled out her cellphone and dialed *911*.

"What are you doing?" Rider asked.

She held the phone to her ear. "Calling the sheriff. We have to report this. Someone has to pay for damaging your property."

Within minutes, Deputy Nash Grayson pulled up in his service vehicle and jumped out. "Wow."

"You don't have to be polite," Selena muttered.

Nash turned to his brother. "Who'd you piss off?"

"I've made it a point since I've been back to keep my head down and my nose clean," Rider said.

Selena shook her head. "Yesterday, he broke up a fight between Shane Fetterlein and Raul Jemenez."

"Oh, yeah. The fight that was over when I arrived." Nash took out a pad and a pen and wrote down the names. "Do you think one of them could have done this?"

Rider shrugged his shoulders. "I really can't say. I didn't see it happen, so I can't name names. However, we did just have a confrontation with Raul at the Ugly Stick Saloon just a few minutes ago."

Selena's eyes narrowed. "He could have come earlier," she said. She glanced around. "Town's pretty deserted right now. Most everyone we know is out at the Ugly Stick Saloon bidding on cowboys.

"That would account for most of the women of Hellfire," Nash murmured.

"I understand the men who didn't get selected for the auction have joined forces at the community center to play some serious Texas Hold 'em Poker," Nash said. "I'll swing by and see if Shane Fetterlein is one of the players. And I'll ask what time he showed up to play."

"In the meantime, what do you want me to do with this?" Rider asked.

"Leave it as it is," Nash said. "I need to come by in the daytime to get pictures before you attempt to clean or paint over it."

Nash went ahead and shot some photographs using the headlights from both vehicles but promised to get more images in the morning. He left a few moments later to run by the community center to see who was there and ask questions.

Left alone, Selena and Rider stood staring at the building and the ugly writing on the wall. Selena moved closer and slipped her hand into Rider's and squeezed. "I'm sorry this happened to you."

"It's just paint." Rider's hand closed around hers, his fingers tightening. "It'll wash off, or I can paint over it. Either way, it's not permanent."

"Well, I hope it doesn't make you change your mind about staying in Hellfire."

He sighed. "I guess I remember Hellfire as being a friendly little town where people got along."

Selena chuckled. "Most of the time it is. But we aren't perfect. You saw how that worked out yesterday."

"I'm not going to let a little paint make me feel like I need to leave. I find that in most cases there's just one or two people who make it miserable for the majority, and I won't be bullied."

"And I'm sure the majority are glad you're back in Hellfire," Selena said. She leaned into his shoulder. "I, for one, am glad you're back."

Rider slipped his arm around her shoulder and pulled her close. "Me, too." He turned her in his arms and stared down into her eyes in the glow of the headlights. "For the record, Raul is wrong. There's no difference between the Sanchezes and the Graysons. We're all people. We all live in the same place. We're allowed to love whomever we want. I just want you to know that." He stared down at her for a long time, and then slowly lowered his face until his lips hovered above hers.

Selena couldn't resist the pull. She tilted her face upward until her lips were a breath away from his. She knew it was wrong. She knew she was tempting fate. But she couldn't resist Rider Grayson.

And when he did kiss her, it was everything she could have imagined and more. She gasped, opening her mouth to his. His tongue slid in and caressed hers in a long, slow, sexy glide. Selena's knees wobbled. She rested her hands against his chest and leaned into him, deepening the connection.

The kiss seemed to go on forever, and yet it ended way too soon.

When Rider lifted his head, Selena closed her eyes and drew in a deep breath. She ran her tongue across her lips, tasting him again. "You know you don't owe me anything for bidding on you at the auction. It was your money. You don't owe me a date or anything else."

"When I kissed you, owing you anything was the furthest thing from my mind," Rider said. Then he bent and kissed her again.

Again, Selena had no will to resist. She fell into him with her entire heart.

CHAPTER 5

AFTER PULLING BACK from the kiss, Rider kept her his arms, but stared at the paint on the wall of his garage. Anger rose again, not so much because of the paint and all the cleaning he'd have to do to get it off, but because of Selena's reaction. He didn't want her to worry.

"Do you want me to take you back out to the ranch to stay the night?" Selena asked.

"No, I'll be fine here." Rider turned to Selena. "Let's get you to your apartment before I call it a night."

Selena looked up at him. "I don't need you to come with me to my apartment."

"After seeing this, I'd feel better making sure you're safe." Rider refused to take no for an answer.

Selena's jaw tightened. "I can take care of myself."

"I know you can. But I'd feel better knowing

everything's okay at your apartment." He sighed. "If it makes you feel better, you can drive over there by yourself. But I'll jog along and be there before you, cutting through the streets. Or take my bike and follow along behind."

Selena shook her head, frowning. "Don't be ridiculous. Get in the car."

They both climbed into her vehicle and drove the two and a half blocks to Selena's apartment over Lola Engel's garage.

The moment the headlights shone on the apartment over the garage, Selena gasped.

Rider's jaw hardened. On the garage and on the stairs leading up to her apartment were the words, *Go BACK to Mexico Whore.*

Another car pulled in behind Selena's, and Rider turned to see Lola jump out of her MG Midget.

"Holy shit! Who did that?" Lola asked.

"Probably the same person who spray-painted the front of Rider's garage," Selena muttered.

Lola turned to Rider. "Somebody tagged you, too?"

Rider nodded. "I don't like this." He tipped his head toward the stairs. "Let's go look and make sure nothing's damaged inside."

Selena led the way up the stairs, followed by Rider and then Lola.

After Selena unlocked the door and pushed it

inward, Rider stepped around her into the room and switched on the light.

Inside, the area was as neat as a pin. It didn't take long for Rider to inspect the studio apartment where the bedroom, living room, and kitchen were all one big room. The only separate room was the bathroom. He turned to Selena. "Anything out of place?" he asked.

Selena shook her head. "No, everything looks just as I left it a couple hours ago."

Lola whistled. "Wow, I don't think I've seen this place this neat, since—well, since forever." She tipped her head toward Selena. "How did the cookies go over?"

Selena's cheeks reddened.

Rider chuckled. "They were great. Did you help Selena make them?"

Lola held up her hands. "Oh, Lord no. My talents don't run in the baking world. Now ask me what shoe goes with any kind of outfit, and I'm your girl."

Selena grimaced at her landlady. "Well it looks as though all the damage is relegated to the exterior of the building. None inside."

Rider shook his head slowly. "Still, I don't feel comfortable with you staying here alone. What if the *artist* returns?"

"I can fend off a man armed with a can a spray paint."

Rider hiked his eyebrows. "What if he's armed with more than paint?"

Lola smiled. "She's welcome to stay with me in the big house. I wouldn't mind having the company."

Rider glanced at Selena. He wasn't convinced she'd be any safer with Lola. But considering his garage had been as damaged as Selena's apartment, he didn't feel confident that staying with him would be any safer.

Selena shook her head. "I'll be all right in the apartment. Again, it was just spray paint."

Rider frowned. "I don't know. It was a pretty threatening statement. Paint now, but who know what comes later?"

Lola slipped an arm around Selena's shoulders. "Don't borrow trouble, Rider." She squeezed Selena's shoulders and smiled up at Rider. "She'll be all right at my place. And I have an HK-40 that I'm licensed to carry concealed."

A chill raced down Rider's spine. "And that's supposed to make me feel better?"

Lola's lips twisted. "I know how to use it. I've taken it to the range on multiple occasions. I'm a crack shot, actually."

Rider gazed into Selena's eyes. "Selena?"

Selena nodded. "Okay. If it'll make you feel better, I'll stay at Lola's house."

Lola laughed. "Well, your enthusiasm makes me feel all warm inside."

Selena grimaced and smiled up at Lola. "No, really, thank you for the offer. I just prefer to be independent. I do appreciate staying with you—just for tonight, though."

Lola squeezed her shoulders again and let go. "Well then, that's settled. What do you want me to carry over that you'll need tonight?"

"I can manage that. Just need my PJs and toothbrush. I can shower in the morning," Selena said.

Lola gave Rider a direct glance. "You don't have to wait for us, if you need to get home."

"If it's all the same to you," Rider crossed his arms over his chest, "I'd like to see that both of you make it over to your house just fine."

Lola shrugged. "Suit yourself."

A moment later, Selena, PJs and toothbrush in hand, followed Lola over to her house. Rider saw them to the door and inside.

"If you want to check the house over to make sure there's no bogeyman under the beds, you're welcome to." Lola stepped aside and allowed Rider to enter the house.

He made a quick search of the entire house, looking in closets and under beds, just as Lola had suggested. When he returned, Lola was grinning and Selena frowning.

"The coast is clear," Rider said.

"Why, thank you," Lola said. "It appears chivalry is not dead."

When he turned to leave, Selena touched his arm. "Are you going to be all right going back to your garage? Maybe you should stay the night at the ranch."

Rider shook his head. "It was just paint." He cupped her face with one hand. "Besides, I have a Glock 9MM pistol under my pillow I sleep with every night. And I know how to use it," he said, glancing over Selena's shoulder to Lola with a grin.

Lola returned his grin. She winked and turned away. "I'll leave you two to your goodbyes."

Selena hurriedly said, "Oh, that's all right. Um, we have nothing to say."

"Uh huh." Lola gave them a smirky grin. "I can see that." She turned and left the room, anyway.

"Thank you for bidding on me at the auction," Rider said.

Selena smiled up at him. "I didn't do anything. I just spent your money."

"Well, I owe you dinner for saving me from Mrs. Cleyburne's clutches." He stared down into her eyes. "So, tomorrow night?"

Selena's eyes widened. "You really don't have to."

"Yes, I do." Rider bent and brushed his lips across hers. "Really, I do." Then he stepped back.

Before she could form any thoughts in her scrambled brain, he crossed to the door.

"Close the door and lock it behind me." He left Lola's house, pulling the door closed with a soft click. He waited until he heard the snick of the lock behind him before he left. Then he walked the two and a half blocks back to his garage apartment, wondering what had made him kiss Selena. But more importantly, wondering why he was so glad he had.

Once he was back at his apartment, Rider wandered from room to room, taking note of the few possessions he still retained after his divorce. He had a loveseat his ex-wife couldn't stand. A small dinette table he had found at a yard sale, and a sofa table behind the love seat that he'd also found at a yard sale.

On that sofa table was a photograph from his childhood that he'd kept with him all this time. It was a picture his mother had taken when he, his brothers, his sister Lily, Kinsey Phillips, and Selena had all gone on a horseback ride, carrying a picnic with them. They'd headed out to the creek and played in the water, and then rode like the wind back to the house when it had started getting dark.

That day was one of his happiest memories, and he'd carried that photograph with him everywhere he'd gone. At one point, his ex-wife had him put it away in his nightstand because it didn't match their décor. Well, it didn't match his décor anywhere, but it matched what was in his heart. He'd missed his family. He'd missed his friends. He'd missed Hellfire. But now that he was home, it was apparent that someone did not want him there and would rather that he went back to Dallas.

The first couple of months he'd been home, he'd spent time setting up his business and building a clientele of people whose cars he'd fixed. Word of mouth had spread the news that he was in business and was pretty decent at fixing engines and changing tires. Now that he was established, and the dust had settled with his divorce, he found himself with more time on his hands. He had spent some of that time watching the market, trading stock and looking for good sales and better buys.

Lately, he'd found himself restless. Wanting more. Was he lonely? Had pulling Selena out of the fight the day before brought back old memories to haunt him? If so, why did he bother chasing them? He couldn't recapture his youth or the fun they'd had as children. Selena was a grown woman now with a path of her own that didn't coincide with his. If he was smart, he would cancel their dinner date for the next night.

But he wasn't smart. He wanted that time with Selena. He knew she'd be leaving soon, and he'd miss her when she was gone. But he wanted that time with her now.

What bothered him was that his connection to Selena might be causing problems for her as well. Whoever had targeted him with the graffiti on the outside of his garage had also taken that graffiti to Selena's apartment. Was somebody striking back at him for having an interest in the beautiful Hispanic woman? He could understand if Raul had sprayed the graffiti paint on his garage but didn't believe Raul would ever paint *Go Back to Mexico Whore* on Selena's apartment. Perhaps it had been Shane Fetterlein who had sprayed the graffiti both places. He had reason to attack them both after Selena and Rider had broken up the fight between Shane and Raul. Yeah, it made more sense that Shane had done the graffiti. He hoped his brother, Nash, would know who was responsible after his visit to the poker game at the community center.

About the time that he decided to call his brother, his own cellphone rang. He glanced down at the screen to see that Nash was calling. He answered on the first ring.

"Yo, bro. What'd ya find out?" he asked.

"Shane Fetterlein was at the community center for most of the evening. He left maybe thirty minutes before I arrived."

"Would that have given him time to come by my place and spray paint my walls, and then hit Selena's place as well?"

"Someone painted Selena's apartment, too?" Nash asked.

Rider explained what they'd found on Selena's apartment. "I was going to tell you about it. I was waiting for you to call back, once you'd talked to Shane."

"Wish I'd gotten hold of him. I went by his place, but he wasn't there. And then I drove out to the Ugly Stick Saloon, because of an altercation in the parking lot."

"Did you have some cowboys fighting?" Rider asked.

"No, actually, it was a couple of women fighting over one of the cowboys. Apparently, one woman won the bid, and the other one was angry about it. She picked a fight with the woman who won." Nash chuckled.

"Did you get in the middle of a cat fight?"

"Are you kidding?" Nash's tone suggested he thought Rider had lost his mind. "I called for backup. Once backup arrived, we split the two women and took them off to different holding cells. They'll sleep it off. Hey, and what's this I hear about Selena winning you in the cowboy auction?"

Rider grimaced. "Good news travels fast, doesn't it?"

"Yes, it does in a small town," Nash said. "I didn't know you had a thing for Selena."

Rider's chest tightened. He hadn't known he had one for her either. "Who said I have a thing for Selena?"

"Well, why would she bid on you if you didn't? That'd be awkward."

"Look, I did as someone suggested at dinner last night. I funded the money for my bid. And I had

Selena do the bidding for me. That's it. Nothing else."

"Nothing, huh?" Nash chuckled again. "And you guys were laying outside, watching the stars, because there's nothing between you, right?"

"They're just stars. So, sue us."

"Just stars, huh? Were you holding her hand to keep her from falling out of the lounge chair?" Nash laughed out loud. "Don't worry. Your secret's safe with me."

Rider's hand tightened on his phone. "What secret?"

"That you're back on the market," Nash said. "Don't worry. I won't mention it. But I'm glad to see you didn't let your divorce turn you against women."

"I'm not on the market." The thought of jumping back into the dating pool made Rider cringe.

Nash snorted. "You mean to tell me you're not taking Selena out on the date you promised when she bid for her cowboy?"

"Well…" Rider hedged. "It's not exactly a date. It's a promise I made because she did a favor for me."

"Well, whatever you're calling it," Nash said, "Selena's a nice girl. Don't break her heart."

"Hey, Nash." Rider hesitated. "If one of us were to fall for the daughter of someone who works for the family, you wouldn't see anything wrong with that, would you?"

"Ha!" Nash said. "It's like I thought. You do have a

thing for Selena."

"I didn't say that," Rider said. "But, if one of us were to fall for somebody like Selena, it's not wrong, is it? I mean, her father works for our father. Would it be weird?"

"Rider, did you spend too long in Dallas with those stuck-up debutantes?"

"No, but apparently Selena thinks she doesn't fit in our circle. That she doesn't belong with a Grayson."

"Where did she get a crazy idea like that?"

"I don't know, but all through our lives, every time we asked Pedro and Margarita to join us at the table, they always said they'd already eaten. However, when we'd go into the kitchen, we'd find them eating their dinner there."

"Yeah, I thought that was odd," Nash said. "Until the other night, when you got up and joined them in kitchen, and then the whole family joined them. It just seemed right."

Rider nodded even though his brother couldn't see him. "The Sanchezes have been at the ranch for longer than I can remember. In fact, I think they were there when most of us were born. Hell, I remember when Selena was born, and Mrs. Sanchez brought her to the ranch. They're like family to us. I don't know why she'd think she doesn't belong with us."

"Do you think her father had something to do

with that?" Nash asked.

"Could be," Rider said. "But how do you undo the training of a lifetime?"

"If Selena is the person you want, you'll have to work hard to make her realize there can be something between you two."

"Again, I'm not dating Selena. I'm just asking a rhetorical question." Rider knew his brother could see right through him, but he didn't want to argue the point.

"Okay then, I hope you and Selena enjoy your not-really-a-date of a date when you do have it."

"We're going tomorrow night," Rider said.

"Ha!" Nash said. "Thought she couldn't resist. Don't worry. I won't bring it up at the family dinner. Again, your secret is safe with me. But, Hellfire is a small town. Word will get out if you stay in Hellfire."

"Maybe we'll go someplace besides Hellfire. Maybe we'll go to Hole in the Wall or a county over."

"That might be your best bet," Nash said. "In the meantime, I'll let you know whatever I find out—if I ever catch up with Shane Fetterlein."

"Thanks, Nash," Rider said.

After hanging up on his brother, Rider paced the length of his apartment several times, worrying about Selena and Lola. He couldn't settle down to sleep, and television didn't hold his interest. Finally, he gave up, pulled on a T-shirt and headed back to Lola's.

CHAPTER 6

S<small>ELENA</small> S<small>TOOD</small> in the doorway of Lola's spare bedroom, staring at the queen-size bed covered in a froth of lace and ruffles.

"I know it's a little girly and froufrou, but Mr. Engel and I had always hoped we'd have a little girl." Lola shrugged. "Children were just not in the cards. And when Mr. Engel died, I didn't have the heart to change the comforter and curtains."

Selena touched her landlady's arm, her heart pinching hard in her chest. "Lola, I'm sorry for your loss. Mr. Engel seemed like a very nice man. He always smiled and had nice things to say to anybody he met on the street."

Lola smiled. She stared into the distance as if staring into the past. "Mr. Engel was every woman's dream come true. Handsome, romantic, loving and considerate. I was lucky to have him for as long as I did. I miss the man," she said. After a long pause, she drew in a deep breath and let it go. "But he's been gone now for five years. He would've wanted me to move on and find a new man in my life. He knew how much love I had in my heart to give."

"And have you found somebody you'd like to spend your life with?" Selena asked.

"There are a couple of guys I wouldn't mind fooling around with. But no, I haven't found anyone I would want to spend the rest of my life with like Mr. Engel. I don't think that man exists."

"Do you believe there's only one true mate for each individual out there?" Selena asked.

"Mm, not necessarily," Lola said. "But maybe, for me, Mr. Engel was the only one. I haven't found anybody who measures up to his standard."

"What if the one you fall in love with doesn't return the same love?" Selena asked.

Lola pressed a hand to her chest. "Ah, unrequited love." She sighed again. "Honey, sometimes you just have to go after what you want. Life is way too short to worry about the little things. Go for the big stuff. You like Rider, don't you?" Lola winked. "It's pretty obvious."

Selena's eyebrows rose, and her mouth dropped open. "Seriously? You think I'm referring to him? And me?" She shook her head. "He just got out of a bad marriage, and I'm on my way to school in January. No, I was just wondering."

"Well, the room's all yours," said Lola. "The bathroom's down the hall. Yell if you need anything from me. Otherwise, I'll be sleeping with my HK-40 under my pillow and listening for any kind of noise in case something goes bump in the night."

Selena laughed as she expected Lola would want her to. When the older woman turned and walked down the hall, Selena entered the bedroom and closed the door. Though the bed looked like something only a woman would sleep in, Selena couldn't help thinking about what Rider would look like lying amongst the frilly comforter and pillow shams. The pink and green ruffles would do nothing to detract from Rider's masculinity. Her lips still tingled from the kiss he'd given her before he'd left. Selena wondered whether his lips were tingling as well. She doubted it, but it didn't hurt to dream.

After she turned back the blankets, she fluffed the pillows and stared down at the bed. Maybe it would be a good idea to get a cool shower before she laid down. She gathered her PJs and her toothbrush and exited the room to find the bathroom down the hallway. Lola's house was quaint, probably built in the early 1900s, but had been updated with the right amenities, although, she hadn't done anything towards updating the furnishings. In fact, she'd stuck with the early 1900s styles with its solid wood furniture, wall paper, and wainscoting along the hallway. Even in the bathroom, Selena found a claw foot bathtub with a shower curtain strung all the way around it. On the shelf beside the tub were some fragrant bath bombs.

So, instead of a shower, Selena opted for a bath, filling the tub with warm water and one of the bath bombs. The fragrant scent of honeysuckle filled the air in the bathroom. Selena stripped out of her clothes and sank into the tub. It was big enough for two people.

Now, she imagined leaning back against Rider's body—*Rider's naked body*. She piled her hair on her head and secured it with a rubber band, and then sank down beneath the water until her shoulders were covered, letting the scented bath bomb oils cover her skin. She lay for a while, relaxing in the warmth. Letting the stress of the day slide off her. She leaned her head against the porcelain and closed her eyes, trying not to think of anything but the warmth of the water and the scent surrounding her. But that was not to be. Every time she closed her eyes, images of Rider came to mind. And again, she thought of him in the tub, and how she'd lean against him as he smoothed water over her shoulders, arms and breasts, and even lower...to the junction of her thighs.

Selena let her fingers follow the path his took in her imagination until she touched the curls atop her mound. A low moan rose up her throat and escaped into the hollows of the bathroom, echoing off the walls. She clapped a hand over her mouth, her eyes shooting wide open. She prayed her landlady didn't hear her moaning as she sank into the bathtub. Pleasuring one's self was something one did in one's own home, not in her landlady's spare bathroom. What would Lola think if she knew of the thoughts running through her head?

Pushing her naughty thoughts to the back of her mind, Selena enjoyed the bath for a few minutes longer before finally standing, rinsing and drying off. She slipped into the old T-shirt and yoga pants she wore as her PJs. After hanging her towel on a rail, she exited the bathroom, carrying her clothes.

Voices downstairs made her pause in the hallway with her hand on the doorknob to the bedroom she'd been assigned. Lola's laughter floated up the stairway. An answering deep-toned male laugh followed. Selena stood stock-still, waiting for the next sound, wondering to whom the male voice belonged. A moment later, she heard a low rumble she could have sworn was Rider's voice. A ripple of awareness skittered across her skin and sent warmth down to her core.

She tiptoed to the railing overlooking the living room area, but she couldn't see who was there.

Lola appeared at the base of the stairs, her back to Selena as she talked to someone in the living room. "You have a pillow," Lola said, "and if you need another blanket, there are more in the chest in the corner. I hope you sleep well. If you don't need anything else, I'll see you in the morning. Oh, and how do you like your eggs? Over easy or scrambled?"

"Over easy. Thanks, but I can cook for myself when I get back to my apartment."

Selena sucked in a sharp breath. It was Rider's voice she had heard. She backed away as Lola turned to walk up the stairs. She reached her door when Lola topped the landing. Selena pretended like she didn't know that Lola had come up the stairs.

She had her hand on the doorknob, turning it, when Lola said, "Hey." Lola closed the distance between them, and then leaned close to her ear. "I knew he couldn't stay away from you for long." She winked. "I'd say the attraction is pretty mutual. So much for unrequited love." She winked again and walked away. Lola threw a parting comment over her shoulder, "And just so you know, I take a rather large sleeping pill, and I don't hear much of anything in the middle of the night. Just in case you want to make a little noise, I won't hear a thing."

Heat rushed into Selena's cheeks. She pushed through her bedroom door and closed it behind her. Leaning against it, her breathing came in ragged gasps. Rider was downstairs. Rider, the man who'd kissed her just a few moments ago. Rider, the man she'd been dreaming about when she was in the bathtub. Holy smokes, he was downstairs. And she was just feet away from him. She pressed a hand to her chest. Dare she go downstairs and strike up a conversation?

Selena shook her head. No. She shouldn't. Despite Lola's inference, Selena knew Rider was just concerned over their welfare. It didn't mean he was attracted to her. For all she knew he might be attracted to Lola. The older woman was quite a good-looking woman for her age. Any man would find her appealing. A little voice in the back of Selena's head said, *But he didn't kiss Lola. He kissed you.*

Warmth filled her body and warmed her core. If she did go down the stairs, what would she say? She stared at her image in the mirror, her hair piled on top of her head and wearing her old T-shirt and yoga pants. It wasn't like she was a sex kitten on her way down to seduce a Grayson brother. She looked like a kid sister who would hang out with him and talk about old times.

Perhaps that was what she could do. They did have their past in common. All the times they'd ridden together, pretty much as a family. They could talk about that, and she could ask about the cars he was working on and the people he was doing the work for. Heck, they knew everybody in town, so it wouldn't be a stretch to talk about the different people they had grown up with.

Selena loosened the rubber band in her hair and let the tresses fall around her shoulders. She ran her fingers through the strands, straightening them from the mass of tangles. She considered her hair one of her greatest attributes. It was thick, glossy, black and healthy. No, she wasn't a blonde-haired, blue-eyed debutante from Dallas.

But maybe that wasn't what Rider wanted. Having just divorced a blonde-haired, blue-eyed debutante, he might be in more of a mood for a dark-haired, dark-eyed Hispanic girl with more fire in her blood than one of those ice princesses from Dallas.

Nope.

She couldn't just waltz down the stairs and strike up a conversation when all she wanted to do was throw herself into his arms and continue that kiss where it had left off earlier.

Nope.

She couldn't do it.

However, she *was* thirsty. A drink of water was a very good excuse to go downstairs to the kitchen and rummage around for a glass of water, maybe put some ice in it. Make a little noise. And if it happened to make Rider come check it out, well then, she would have an excuse to say a few words to him. *And maybe sneak another kiss.*

Before she could talk herself out of it, she reached for the doorknob, pulled it open, and hurried out of the bedroom and down the stairs. She didn't glance to the side when she passed the living area, but she could see in her peripheral vision where Rider stood by the front living room window. She tiptoed past him to the kitchen, opened the door softly and closed it behind her. Unfamiliar with the kitchen's layout, she switched on the light and rummaged in the cabinets until she found a glass and filled it with ice from the freezer. The squeak of the hinge alerted her to the fact that the kitchen door was opening. She turned the faucet and filled her glass with water. She knew he was there, but he would have to be the first one to acknowledge that he was in the room with her.

"Where'd you get the glass?" Rider asked.

Selena girded her loins and turned with a bright, "Oh, I didn't know you were here."

Rider's lips twisted. "Really? We made enough noise to wake the dead."

Selena shrugged and started to walk past him. "I was in the bath. I didn't realize Lola had company."

He took two steps forward, closing the distance between them. "You mean you didn't come downstairs to see me?"

He stood so close she could smell his aftershave. Selena found herself leaning toward him, inhaling deeply. "Na, nah, nooo, of course not," she said. "Why did you come back?"

He smiled. "For one, I was worried about you and Lola, here, by yourselves. And two, I couldn't stop thinking about that kiss."

Selena's eyes widened. "The kiss?" She'd been thinking about that nonstop since he'd left.

Rider nodded. "The kiss." He took the glass from her hand and set it on the counter. Then he took her arms and pulled her close until their chests touched. His hands slipped up behind her back and threaded into her hair, tipping her head backward. "All I could think about was kissing you again."

Selena's knees wobbled. She settled her hands on his chest. Her fingers curled into his T-shirt. When she should have pushed him away, she found herself whispering, "What are you waiting for?"

His arms closed around her. His lips crushed hers. And he kissed her. Pushing his tongue past her teeth to slide along the length of hers in a long smooth caress.

Selena's arms rose, her hands linking behind his neck pulling him closer. He slid his fingers down her back and cupped her thighs, lifting her and setting her on the counter behind her.

She crossed her ankles behind his back and pulled him close, pressing her sex against the ridge behind the denim of his jeans. As the kiss deepened, he pressed closer to her as if he couldn't get close enough. After a long moment, he raised his head, cupped her cheeks in his hands and stared down at her. "I want to do sooo much more," he said softly, "but this is neither my place nor yours."

Selena brushed a strand of hair off his forehead and leaned close to his ear. "Lola takes a sleeping pill before she goes to bed," she whispered. Then she reached for the hem of his T-shirt and tugged it free of his waistband.

"Would it be wrong to make love to you in another woman's kitchen?" Rider said against her ear.

Selena melted against him, her breathing shallow, her heart pounding. "Lola told me herself, 'Go for what you want. Life's short.'"

Selena pulled the shirt over Rider's head and tossed it to the side. He grabbed the hem of her shirt and lifted it up. She raised her arms over her head and let the shirt slide free of her arms and head. He tossed it across a chair and stared down at her full perky breasts. He cupped each rounded globe in his palms as if weighing them. "You're not the little girl I grew up with."

Selena leaned forward into his cupped hands. "No, I'm quite grown up." And she reached for the button on his jeans, flipped it open, and then guided the zipper down.

His shaft sprang free, and she wrapped her fingers around it. "Quite grown up," she repeated.

Rider slipped his hands into the waistband of her yoga pants and dragged them downward, lifting her off the counter to slip them over her thighs and past her calves and ankles.

Selena pushed his jeans down past his buttocks. Just far enough to where she could cup the rounded globes of his ass. As he pressed the tip of his cock to her entrance, she paused and looked up at him. "Protection?"

He drew in a deep breath and let it out slowly, nodding. "Back pocket."

Selena stretched to reach for the wallet in his back pocket, opened it and found a foil package inside. She dropped his wallet on the counter and tore open the packet. Eagerly, she leaned back far enough to roll the condom down his erection. Then she positioned him at the entrance to her channel, wrapped her ankles around his back and pulled him close.

He paused before entering her. "Are you sure about this?"

She nodded. "More certain about this than anything else in my life."

She tightened her thighs around him, and he eased into her slick channel, filling her, stretching her, making her feel so complete, she could barely breathe.

He drove deeper until he could go no more. And then he paused and waited for her channel to adjust to his girth.

Selena breathed in and out, trying to remember how, when all she wanted to do was rock back and forth. "More, please."

He pulled out, drove back inside, and then settled into a smooth rhythm, in and out, in and out.

The faster he moved, the harder it was for her to

catch her breath. Tingling began deep in her core and spread outward, all the way to her fingertips. Her body shook with the force of her release. And then Rider stiffened, his body coming to a screeching halt. He thrust one last time, burying himself deep inside of her. His body shuddered, and he shook, holding her close, his fingers tight around her hips.

When she could finally breathe again, she leaned her forehead against his chest and chuckled.

Rider tipped up her chin. "What's so funny?"

Selena's chuckled turned into giggles, and she pointed toward the window. "We were so worried about Lola seeing us, we didn't even think about the curtains being open on the kitchen windows." She pressed herself against him.

He lifted her by the backs of her thighs and carried her out of the kitchen and into the living room, where the blinds had been closed and the curtains drawn. There, he laid her on the couch. "Is that better?" he asked.

She wrapped her arms around his neck and pulled him down to kiss her. "Much," she said. Selena scooted to the edge of the couch. Leaving enough room for Rider to slide in behind her and spoon her body with his.

Rider wrapped his arms around her and pulled her close. Sliding a blanket over both their naked bodies, he nuzzled the back of her neck and whispered in her ear, "You know, this changes everything, don't you?"

Selena sighed. "Does it have to?"

He pressed his lips to the back of her neck. "Yes, it does."

She yawned and leaned her head against him. "Do you mind if I don't think about it until tomorrow?"

He chuckled. "Not at all. As long as we do talk about it tomorrow."

Selena nodded, letting her eyes drift closed. Tomorrow was another day, but tonight was hers, and she'd gone for what she'd wanted. She would have no regrets over what they'd done. But she also knew that it hadn't changed her plans. She was still on track to go to school in January. There was no changing that. As much as she wanted to be with Rider, she had a plan, and she was sticking to it.

CHAPTER 7

RIDER LAY for a long time with Selena nestled in his arms. Sometime in the early morning hours, he rose from the couch and dressed. He lifted Selena and carried her to the room Lola had assigned her. Gently, he laid her down, kissed her lips and pulled a blanket up around her neck. Then he left the house and returned to his apartment.

The sun was just beginning to rise when he arrived in front of the garage. A different car stood in the parking lot from the night before. He recognized it, and his blood ran cold. What the hell was his ex-wife doing there?

He walked past her car and noted that she was sound asleep with her head resting against the back of her seat. He walked past her and up the stairs to his apartment, ignoring the fact she was there. He didn't want to confront her. Not yet. He had a lot to think about after sleeping with Selena.

Rider strode through the door, then turned and locked it securely. He stripped out of his clothes and walked into the shower. Once he finished his shower, he dressed in jeans and a T-shirt and pulled on his boots. He ate a quick breakfast and went down to his garage to start work on the vehicles he had contracted to fix.

He was tempted to call the sheriff's department and have his ex-wife's vehicle towed away, with her in it. He could just imagine how mad she would be, but he was even madder over the fact she'd shown up in Hellfire, when she'd never wanted to come to this town the entire time they'd been married. He bet his lack of response to her request for more money was her reason for coming to find him.

As far as he was concerned, their marriage was over; his obligation to fund her lifestyle was complete. He'd given her practically everything that she'd asked for in the divorce. He'd even agreed to pay alimony, even though he knew she had trust funds from her deceased grandparents.

He worked inside the garage with the garage door closed, changing air filters, changing oil and tinkering with the different cars he had up on the lifts. Around nine o'clock in the morning, it started to get warm inside the garage, so he figured it was time to open the big garage door and risk waking his ex. He hit the button for the automatic garage door opener and watched as the door lifted and rolled overhead. And sure enough, his ex was standing there.

She wrinkled her nose and stared around the garage. "Good lord, Rider. You work in this filth?"

He crossed his arms over his chest. "Some people like to work with their hands."

Rider hadn't seen his ex-wife since they'd sat across the table in the lawyer's office and signed the divorce papers. "Hello, Lydia. What are you doing in Hellfire?"

She picked her way around the grease on the floor, careful not to touch anything and get her white pantsuit dirty. "Daddy said he misses you at the firm."

"Your father has plenty of other financial planners at the firm." Rider raised his brows. "Try again."

Lydia stared around the garage with the two cars jacked up on platforms, her nose wrinkling. "I may have made a mistake."

Rider's jaw clenched. "A mistake in coming to Hellfire? Or a mistake in stepping into my garage?"

"No, silly," Lydia said. "I made a mistake about our, you know, our little divorce thingy."

"Our divorce thingy?" Rider looked at her as if she'd grown another head. "Our divorce is final."

Lydia stared across at him. "I know. I was there at the signing. But does it have to be final?" She closed the distance between them and touched her fingertip to his chest. "I mean, we once were in love."

Rider grabbed her finger and moved it away from his chest. Lydia pulled her hand back and studied it as though looking for grease spots.

"You have to admit," Rider said. "What love we might have felt for each other was long gone by the time you decided to sleep with my partner."

Lydia pressed her pretty pink lips together in a tight line. "Are you going to hold that against me forever?"

"Lydia, you cheated on me." Rider shook his head. "Where I come from, people don't forgive cheating. There's a reason for the cheating. At least one of the people involved no longer loves the other person. Lydia, I don't think you ever truly loved me."

"Of course, I loved you, Rider." Lydia walked toward him again, her hand outstretched.

Rider backed away, holding his hand up. "Don't touch me, Lydia. You'll get your hands dirty."

"But, Rider, darling," Lydia said, "I want you to come home to me."

Rider shook his head. "This is my home, Lydia. I told you a long time ago that I wanted to come back to Hellfire. You didn't want to come. Are you telling me you want to come now?"

Lydia looked around the garage again and shook her head. "Of course not. I want you to come back to Dallas with me."

"Why, Lydia?" Rider demanded. "Did your daddy cut you off from the trust fund?"

"Daddy's got this silly thought in his head that I need to go to work for his firm."

"You mean, your father's finally going to make you work for your money?"

Lydia sucked in a deep breath and let it out on a huff. "Daddy doesn't understand that I don't get the numbers games."

"Your daddy has a business to run. He just wants you to understand how money is made and how best to spend it."

"I know how to spend money. It's making it that has me baffled."

"Lydia, what you need is to go to work for a minimum wage job to understand exactly how much it takes to live on a minimum wage salary. Then perhaps, you'd understand more about the amounts you spend on your shoes."

"And what's wrong with my shoes? "Lydia stared down at the white pumps she wore with her white suit and made a face. "Oh dear, look, there's a little black spot on my shoe." She pulled a tissue from her small designer handbag and bent to dab at the dot on her white shoe. The dot smeared into a line, and she grimaced. "Now, look at what you've done," she whined. "My shoe is ruined."

"Lydia, I didn't ask you to come to Hellfire." Rider

tipped his head toward the garage door. "Go home to Dallas. Go home to your daddy, Lydia."

Lydia frowned. "Does this have anything to do with the woman who bid for you at the auction last night?"

Rider frowned. "What do you know about the auction?"

Lydia shrugged. "I might have been there..." She ran her gaze from the top of his head to the tip of his boots. "I never expected to see Rider Grayson strutting his stuff on a stage with a lot of women hooting and hollering like heathens."

"The auction was to raise money for the children of the tri-county area." Rider said.

"I get that. I'm not stupid," Lydia said.

From Rider's perspective, Lydia was not stupid when it came to manipulation and working people. She may not understand numbers and where money came from, but she was not stupid when it came to dealing with people. "Lydia, the auction had nothing to do with you," Rider said.

Lydia's eyes narrowed. "So, the woman who bought you is nothing but a stranger?"

"I didn't say that," Rider said.

Lydia's eyes narrowed to slits. "Then she does mean something to you," Lydia said as a statement, not as a question.

"If she means something to me," Rider said, "that has absolutely nothing to do with you."

Lydia crossed her arms over her chest. "You're saying I mean nothing to you, after all the time we were married?"

"Obviously, I meant nothing to you, Lydia," Rider said. "Otherwise you wouldn't have slept with my partner."

Her expression crumpled. "But, Rider, I was lonely. You were never home. What was a girl supposed to do?"

Rider had to admit that he'd worked late hours many nights, trying to prove himself as a financial planner in her father's firm. But that hadn't given her the right to fool around in his bed, with his partner. "Lydia, the point is, we are divorced."

Lydia touched her fingers to his chest. "But it doesn't have to be that way."

Rider took her hand in his and pulled it away from his chest. "Yes, it does."

"But I don't want to be divorced."

"It's too late, Lydia," Rider said. "What's done is done. I have no desire to be married to you anymore. I have no love left for you."

"Oh, Rider, you don't mean that." Lydia slipped one of her hands around his neck. "There has to be some little flicker of love still left inside."

Rider shook his head. "Nope."

Lydia wrapped her other hand around the back of his neck. "Are you sure about that?"

"Absolutely positive," Rider said in clear concise

words.

"Kiss me," Lydia said. She leaned up on her toes and pressed her lips against his.

With Lydia's lips pressed against his, Rider could only think about Selena and how different the two women were. Where Selena was curvy, warm and passionate, Lydia was cold, stiff and annoying.

He didn't want the kiss. He hadn't asked for the kiss. But he suffered it to prove to himself that he really did have no more feelings for Lydia.

He'd much rather be kissing Selena.

The sound of metal clattering against concrete outside the garage made him push Lydia away and look around. A movement caught his eye, but he couldn't tell who it was or where they were going. When he tried to push Lydia away, she clung to him, holding her ground and refusing to let him set her aside.

"Oh, come on, Rider," Lydia said. "You know you love me. You can't stop loving a person that quickly."

"Lydia, I didn't stop loving you that quickly. It happened over time." He set her away from him and turned her toward the door, giving her a gentle push. "Go back to Dallas."

She turned back to him. "But I can't go back," she frowned. "Daddy will make me work."

"Is that all I am to you?" Rider asked. "A way to pay your bills and let you live in the lifestyle to which you've become accustomed?"

"But, Rider, honey, the alimony doesn't go far enough. I can't afford my penthouse apartment on such a paltry amount."

"Then move, Lydia." Rider picked up a greasy oil can and held it between him and Lydia as a shield.

It was effective. Lydia maintained a distance between the oil can and her white pant suit. "But I can't move to another apartment. The penthouse is where I live. What would my friends think?"

"They might think that you're divorced now, and that you might have to live a little more within your means." Rider had a hard time feeling sorry for the woman. "Lydia, you got everything you're going to get out of me in the divorce decree. I'm paying you alimony for another year, and then you're on your own. I recommend you either get a job as your father has suggested, or you find another husband willing to support you and your lifestyle."

Lydia stomped her foot. "But my daddy likes you." She frowned. "You won't change your mind, will you? You came back to Hellfire because of her, didn't you?" Lydia stared at him.

"I don't know what you're talking about. I came back to Hellfire, because it's my home." Rider pointed to the door. "Go home, Lydia. You don't belong in Hellfire. You never wanted to come here. I don't know why you're here now."

"I came to bring you back to your senses," Lydia sneered. "You belong in Dallas. You're wasting your talents here in Hellfire. I mean, really, a grease monkey?" She looked around the garage with obvious distaste marring her brow.

"You see it as wasting my talents. I see it as using my talents." Again, Rider pointed toward the door. "Lydia, we never had anything in common, face it. We weren't meant to be together. Go back to Dallas and forget about me. Find yourself a new husband. Find yourself a new life. Or get a job. You might like it."

Lydia snorted, a very un-ladylike sound. "I should have known you had another woman in your life. Had I known that, I would have asked for more money in the divorce decree."

Tired of the discussion, Rider hooked Lydia's arm with his hand and marched her toward the door.

"Un-hand me," she said. She jerked her arm loose from his grip and stared down at the grease marks he'd left on her white jacket. "Now, see what you've done? You stained my suit."

"You're trespassing, Lydia. Leave before I call the sheriff and have him escort you out of my shop."

Lydia harrumphed. "Well, I've never been treated this disrespectfully."

"Well, maybe someone should have. Then maybe you'd get the hint you're not welcome."

Lydia lifted her chin. "You'll be sorry."

"I'm sorry I let our marriage last as long as it did." Again, Rider reached for her arm.

Lydia stepped away and outside of the shop. "This isn't over."

Rider shook his head. "Yes, it is, Lydia." He glanced at a shiny tin lying on the ground beside the shop door. It looked just like the one Selena had brought the day before, filled with cookies. His heart constricted in his chest when he realized Selena must have been there earlier while he was talking with Lydia. He wondered if she'd seen Lydia kiss him. That thought made him want to get rid of Lydia even more.

"Lydia, go away." Rider pointed toward her car. "Now."

Lydia opened her mouth to protest.

Rider raised his hand. "Just go. Not another word."

Lydia pressed her lips together, turned and walked away. After she climbed into her car and drove off, Rider realized he had some damage control to do.

Lydia drove out of the parking lot, into the street, made a U-turn and drove straight back toward the garage, aiming straight at Rider. Rider had been so engrossed in his thoughts about Selena he didn't realize until the last minute what Lydia was doing. As her car bumped up on the curb and raced toward him, he flung himself to the side and rolled to his feet.

Lydia's car hit one of the other vehicles he had

been working on, knocking it off the jacks, onto its metal wheels.

"Are you crazy?" Rider shouted.

Lydia rolled her window down. "Admit it, Rider Grayson. You love this place more than you ever loved me."

"You're right, Lydia," Rider said. "I never loved you as much as I love my home. Now, leave. I'm calling the police." He pulled out his phone and dialed his brother's number. When Nash answered, he spoke loud enough for Lydia to hear. "I'd like to report a trespasser and an attack with a deadly weapon."

Lydia glared, shifted into reverse and backed out of the parking lot. The bumper on her Audi hung loose and scratched against the pavement. Banged-up bumper and all, she drove out of Hellfire and hopefully back to where she belonged.

"Hey, Rider, what's happening?" Nash asked.

Rider had forgotten that he'd dialed his brother's number. "Just had a visit from the ex."

Nash chuckled. "I bet that was pleasant."

"Put her on your list of suspects for the spray paint job," Rider said.

Nash whistled. "You think she might have done it?"

"I wouldn't put it past her," Rider said. "She is one angry bitch."

CHAPTER 8

WHEN THE ALARM on her watch had gone off that morning, Selena had stretched between the sheets, feeling the cotton slide across her naked skin. Sun shone through the window warming her body, reminding her of the heat she and Rider had created between them the night before.

A smile spread across her lips even as she felt the empty bed beside her. Rider being gone didn't bother her. She had a vague memory of him carrying her up the steps and laying her on the bed in the wee hours of the morning. He had laid her on the bed and kissed her gently before closing the door behind him as he'd left. The man was enough of a gentleman to save her the embarrassment of being caught naked on Lola's couch in the morning.

Knowing she had less than an hour to get ready for work, she still couldn't help lingering in the bed, reliving the memory of making love with Rider the night before. All her life she had dreamed of kissing Rider and, as she'd gotten older, of making love with him. Last night, all those dreams had come true. Only making love with him had been so much better than she'd imagined.

Fully awake, she couldn't wait to see him again. She tossed the blankets aside, sat up in bed and swung her legs over the side. In less than a minute, she was dressed in the clothes she'd worn the night before, pulled her shoes on and gathered all her things to carry to the apartment over the garage. As quietly as she could, she left the bedroom and tiptoed down the stairs toward the front entryway.

She was reaching for the doorknob when a voice called out, "Good morning, Selena." Lola stood at the entry to the kitchen. She held up a pair of panties that were obviously Selena's. "I found these in the kitchen. They aren't mine, so unless Rider has a thing for wearing ladies' underwear, I'm assuming they're yours." She grinned from ear to ear. "I suppose your night went so much better than you'd planned."

Heat rose in Selena's cheeks as she took the panties from Lola's hand. "Sorry about that."

Lola shrugged. "I'm just glad somebody's getting some. I don't suppose you'd share all the juicy details with a lonely old widow."

More heat rushed into Selena's cheeks, and she shook her head. "Sorry. I don't kiss and tell."

"Well, it doesn't hurt to ask," Lola said. "I do like to live vicariously when I can't get a man in my bed."

"Lola, honey," Selena said, "you should have no problem whatsoever getting a man in your bed. You're a beautiful woman."

"Oh, I know that," Lola said. "But I'm kind of picky. Lately, I've had my sights set on one man, and one man only."

Selena frowned. "Anybody I know?"

"Oh, I've had my sights set one of the Grayson brothers." Lola held up her hands. "Don't worry. Not Rider."

Selena narrowed her eyes. "You were bidding on Chance Grayson the other night. Is that the Grayson brother you've got your sights set on?"

Lola's smile spread across her face again. "I guess it's no secret I've got the hots for Chance Grayson. But I'm not interested in a long-term relationship. I had that with Mr. Engel, and it was lovely. I don't think I'll ever find a man that I want to spend the rest of my life with. But, a little romp in the bed wouldn't hurt. And a romp in the bed with Chance Grayson would be incredible, I'm sure. What about you?" Lola said. "How did you let Rider get away so early in the morning?"

"I didn't know he'd left." Selena shrugged. "Perhaps he had to get to work early this morning."

"Well, what are you waiting for? The man has to be hungry. And you know how he loves your cookies.

Take him some cookies. What are you waiting for?" Lola shooed her toward the door. "Go get your man."

Glad for the invitation to leave and to avoid any more awkward questions, Selena opened the door and stepped outside into the sunshine. And what a glorious morning it was. She hurried over to her apartment and climbed the stairs, trying to ignore the harsh words spray-painted on the side of the building. She unlocked the door, let herself in and dropped her things on the counter.

Once inside, she hurried to the closet, took out a fresh shirt and jeans and dressed quickly for work at the convenience store. She pulled her hair back into a messy bun, letting some strands fall along the side of her face to soften her appearance. In the kitchenette, she gathered the best of the remaining cookies into a colorful tin. Then she slung her purse over her shoulder, hugged the cookie tin under her arm and stepped out of the apartment.

The sun shone down. The air was cool and smelled of freshly cut grass and honeysuckle. Since the convenience store was only a few blocks away, she usually walked to work. On the way there, she'd pass by Rider's garage. She'd just stop in and drop off the cookies. If they just happened to kiss, well, then so be it.

She set off with a skip in her step and a happy song playing through her head. When she arrived at Rider's garage, she noticed a sleek, expensive red car parked in the parking lot. It wasn't a vehicle she recognized as coming through the convenience store to fill up for gas. She supposed it might belong to an out-of-towner who'd stopped, needing some kind of oil change or tire repair.

With a happy smile on her face, she stepped out of the bright sunshine into the darkness of the garage in time to see a blonde-haired woman throw her arms around Rider's neck and kiss him as if there would be no tomorrow.

Selena stood for a moment in absolute stunned shock. Unable to move. Unable to voice a word. When Rider's hands rose to grip the woman's hips, something inside Selena triggered her to finally move. She dropped the tin and ran from the garage all the way to the convenience store.

When she burst through the shop's door, her boss stepped back from cleaning fingerprints off the glass. "Good morning, Selena. It's going to be a gorgeous day."

Selena blew past him into the store and headed straight for the bathroom. Once inside, she turned, locked the door and faced the mirror. She looked at her reflection, her eyes wide and filled with tears. Pressing her hands to her cheeks, she fought those tears to keep them from falling. But she didn't win that battle. Tears streamed down her cheeks and dripped from her chin into the porcelain sink. Why, oh why, had she thought that she and Rider Grayson would ever be a thing?

He was a Grayson. She was a Sanchez. The blonde-haired woman wearing the designer white suit was more his pace, more his style. Someone who fit better in his world. Selena had just been a distraction along his way. She'd known all this before she'd made love with Rider. And yet, she'd done it anyway. Going for what she wanted, as Lola had insisted.

What she hadn't wanted was the heartbreak and the heartache that went along with it.

As her tears slowed, she looked at her red-rimmed eyes and ducked her head to splash cool water against her face, eyes and cheeks, trying to scrub away all the evidence of her heartbreak. She'd known better. Her father had told her all along she didn't belong in their world. Why hadn't she believed him?

When she had done the best she could to erase the ravages of her tears, she straightened, pushed back her shoulders and left the bathroom to go to work.

Her boss stood behind the counter, waiting on a customer.

As she made her way toward the counter, Selena straightened products on the shelves and on the racks.

By the time she reached the register, the last customer left the building, and her boss looked at her. "What's wrong, Selena?"

She shook her head, the ready tears welling in her eyes again. She could not let them fall.

A single tear trickled down the side of her face.

"Oh, Selena, has some man gone and broken your heart?" Mr. Hutcheson touched her arm. He pressed a tissue into her hand, and said, "If you need time off, take it. I can handle the store today."

Selena shook her head. "No, I'm all right."

And she would be all right. She had a plan to go to school in January. She would become a PA and help people, just as she'd always intended to. With or without Rider Grayson in her life.

The door to the store opened, and Raul Jemenez entered along with a few of his buddies.

Great. Just what I need, Selena thought. A confrontation with Raul.

She turned her back to him and dabbed at the tear streaks on her face. She refused to let him see her cry.

"Selena, *mi amour*," Raul said. "I understand Rider Grayson's wife is in town, and she wants him back."

Selena's heartbeat screeched to a halt and, for a long pause, didn't beat. And then her pulse returned, storming through her veins. So, that had been the woman who'd kissed Rider. And he'd kissed her back.

"I didn't figure he would last long in Hellfire after living in Dallas for all those years," Raul said. "I suppose he'll be heading back to Dallas soon with his wife."

Selena shrugged. "I suppose it's none of our business."

Raul smirked. "You didn't think he'd choose you over her, did you?"

Selena shook her head. "Never. Rider Grayson could have anyone he wants."

"But you didn't think he'd want you, did you?" Raul said, a sneer in his voice.

"I never said he did," Selena said, her heart breaking into a million pieces.

"Good thing you have your head on straight now." Raul shook his head. "For a while there, I thought you had your sights set on the Grayson boy."

"No way," she said, her lips pressing into a tight line. "I've got my sights set on school. And nothing's going to stop me."

"I'm glad you're finally thinking straight," Raul said. "Maybe now, you'd consider going out on a date with me."

Selena shook her head. "No, Raul. I'm not interested in going out with you."

His thick brows descended. "Don't tell me you still think you have a chance with Rider?"

Selena shook her head again. "I'm not that foolish. But I'm also not interested in a date with you, now or ever, Raul."

Raul shrugged his shoulders. "Your loss. But you're not gonna get Rider Grayson. If you'd have seen his wife, you'd realize why. The woman is a knockout. She could be one of those women on that top model television show. She has it all going for her. From the blonde hair to the long legs and perfect clothes." Raul ran his gaze from the top of Selena's head to the tip of her comfortable tennis shoes.

Anger boiled in Selena's veins. "I get the point, Raul. I don't measure up to Grayson standards."

Mr. Hutcheson emerged from the back of the store carrying several bags of ice. His gaze went to Selena and back to Raul. "Good morning, Raul," Mr. Hutcheson said. "I don't suppose you could get the door for me, could you?"

Raul gave Selena one last look before going to the door and opening it for Mr. Hutcheson and his bags of ice.

Mr. Hutcheson exited. "I don't suppose you could also get the door to the ice box too, could you?"

Raul shot another look at Selena. "I'm not giving up."

Selena gave him a grimace. "Raul, you need to. There's nothing between you and me, and there never will be."

Raul left the store to help Mr. Hutcheson open the ice box and deposit his load.

A few moments later, Raul and his friends left the convenience store parking lot on their way to their construction site.

Mr. Hutcheson reentered the store to where

Selena was restocking the candy aisle. "Is Raul the man who put the tears in your eyes?"

Selena shook her head. "No. He isn't."

Mr. Hutcheson sighed. "Well, if he's bothering you, you let me know, and I'll take care of it."

Selena smiled. "Thank you, Mr. Hutcheson. I really appreciate all you do for me."

Her boss patted her back. "You're like a daughter to me, Selena. And I'm very proud of all that you've done, all that you've accomplished, and all that you will accomplish."

"Thank you, Mr. Hutcheson. You don't know how much that means to me."

A shiny red vehicle with a sagging bumper pulled up in front of the store. Selena froze with a wad of candy bars in her hand on its way to the shelf. Mr. Hutcheson's eyes narrowed. "What's wrong?" His gaze traveled to where hers had landed.

A striking woman with blonde hair and blue eyes stepped out of the vehicle in a white pant suit.

"Do you know that woman?" Mr. Hutcheson asked.

"I think that's Rider Grayson's ex-wife." Selena shoved the candy bars onto the shelf. "I think I'll go bag ice if you don't mind, Mr. Hutcheson."

"I've bagged all the ice we'll need today," he said, his gaze shifting between her and the blonde.

"Are there any more boxes in the back that need to be put up on the shelves?" Selena asked.

Mr. Hutcheson shook his head. "Nope, got 'em all put out." His brow dipped low on his forehead. "You want me to take this customer?"

Selena drew in a deep breath and let it go slowly. She might as well face her nemesis. "No, I'll get her."

What had started out as a beautiful morning with the sun shining down, the birds singing and the honeysuckle blooming, filling the air with its lovely fragrance, had turned into more of a nightmare for Selena. She took up a position behind the counter as Rider's ex-wife walked through the door.

The woman stood for a moment glancing around the interior of the store, a frown denting her smooth brow. "What fresh hell have I walked into?" She laughed. "Oh, that's right, I'm in Hellfire, Texas." Her gaze went to Selena behind the counter, and her eyes narrowed. "Do you have anything for a massive headache?" She pressed her fingers to her temples. "In this godforsaken town, there has to be something."

Selena reached behind the counter for a twin pack of ibuprofen and laid it on the counter. "Yes, ma'am," Selena said. She pasted half a smile on her face. "Is that all you need?"

The woman snorted. "Of course, that's not all I need," she snapped. "I'll need something to take it with."

"The refrigerator in the back has sodas, water,

beer and wine." Selena waved toward the rear of the building. "Take your pick."

For a moment, the woman stood there as if she expected Selena to go find whatever she wanted to drink. Then she harrumphed and marched back to the refrigerator and selected a bottled water. She returned to the front, plopped the bottle on the counter and pulled a credit card from her purse. Selena rang up the items and gave her the total. The woman slid the credit card in the card reader and waited. A moment later, the charge on the credit card was declined. Selena glanced up at the woman. "I'm sorry, ma'am. The charge was declined."

"Damn him to hell." She rifled through her wallet and pulled out another credit card and slid it through the card reader. Again, the card was declined.

"Want me to try?" Selena asked.

The woman slapped the card into Selena's hand. "Yes."

Selena ran the card through the reader on the register at the same time noting the name on its plastic surface.

Lydia Grayson.

Though Selena had suspected the woman was Rider's ex-wife, seeing her name made her back stiffen and her guard go up.

After she'd gone through three different credit cards Lydia finally turned her purse upside down and shook the change out of the bottom, muttering as she thumbed through the coins. "Daddy just doesn't understand. It's not as easy as he thinks. If Rider hadn't signed those papers, I would have changed things." She threw her hands in the air and stood back. "Is that enough?"

Selena counted out change enough to pay for the pills and the drink, and then she pushed the rest back toward the woman. Selena deposited the money into the cash register, and then asked Lydia, "Would you like a bag for that?"

Lydia shook her head as she scooped everything off the counter back into her purse. "No, but if you could open the package with the headache medicine, I would appreciate that."

Selena did as she was asked and tore the pills free from the package. She dropped them into Lydia's open palm.

Rider's ex unscrewed the cap from the water bottle and downed the two pills. When she finally put the cap back on the bottle, she looked at Selena across the counter. Her eyes narrowed, and she studied Selena, as if seeing her for the first time. Her lips tightened. "You," she said. "You're the woman who won the bid for Rider Grayson last night."

Selena fought the urge to squirm. She had nothing to squirm about. The money wasn't hers. Rider had asked her to bid for him so that he wouldn't have to go on a date with any other woman in the building. Lydia Grayson did not have to know that. Rider's ex-wife didn't have to know anything about what had happened between Selena and Rider.

"Is that all you need?" Selena asked, pasting a fake smile on her face.

Lydia's gaze swept her from head to toe, and her lips curled back in a sneer. "You know he's married, don't you?"

Selena's brows rose. "From what I understand, he's officially divorced."

Lydia's chin rose. "That's only a formality. He doesn't belong here in Hellfire. He belongs in Dallas…with me."

"Really? Does Rider know this?" She cocked her brows. "From what he's told his family, he intends on staying in Hellfire."

Lydia snorted. "You paid a lot of money for one date with a cowboy, but that's as far as it will go. One date. In fact, I really doubt he'll live up to the promise of that one date. He's coming back to me. He'll be back in Dallas. You just watch. You might as well call off the date. It won't lead to anything else."

Selena forced the smile to remain on her face, and she stared Lydia in the eyes. "I don't care if it's just one date. I don't care if we have wild monkey sex. It's one date with Rider Grayson. And you won't be on it." She tipped her chin toward the door. "Now, if you will excuse me, I have other customers."

Lydia snorted, spun on her heel, and marched toward the door. When she reached it, she turned back and glared at Selena. "You're not the kind of woman Rider Grayson will commit to. At the best, you'll be just a fling," Lydia said.

Selena met her gaze, tipping her chin just a little bit higher. "Apparently, you're not the kind of woman Rider Grayson commits to either." She tipped her head to the side. "Thus, the divorce."

"I told you that was just a formality," Lydia said. "He'll come back to me. Mark my words." And she left the store, letting the door swing shut with a hard slam behind her.

Selena waited until the red sports car with the drooping bumper sped away before she sagged against the counter. All her energy drained from her.

Mr. Hutcheson slipped an arm around her. "I take it Rider Grayson is the man behind the tears."

Selena nodded. "Yeah. He is. But I'm done crying."

"So, are you going on that date with Rider?" He raised his brows. "After all, you did win the bid."

If she were smart. Selena would say, *Oh, hell no.* Instead, she found her mouth opening and the words coming out, "Hell yeah, I'm going on that date." If for no other reason than to prove Lydia wrong.

CHAPTER 9

BASED on the cookie tin Rider had found by the garage door, he figured Selena had been there earlier, about the time that he'd been kissed by his ex-wife. Throughout the day, he'd passed the convenience store where Selena worked and considered stopping in. But each time he'd passed, the convenience store was busy with multiple customers. He didn't want to be interrupted when he had that conversation with Selena about his ex-wife and the fact that his ex-wife had done the kissing, not him.

He saved the explanations for when he came to pick her up for their date later that evening. First, he'd stopped by the florist to pick up a cheerful bouquet of daisies. He wore a nice pair of dark gray trousers, a white button-down shirt and a bolo tie, along with his best cowboy boots, polished to a nice shine. He'd showered and scrubbed all the grease from beneath his fingernails and wore his favorite cologne. He'd spent an hour cleaning his truck, vacuuming and polishing it to a shine. He'd thought of everything he could to make things right with Selena. He had his main plan stashed away in the back seat of his truck for later that evening, if all went well.

First things first, he had to convince Selena to go on the date to begin with. If he were her, he'd tell himself to go to hell. If he'd been the one to walk up on her kissing her ex, he'd have been angry.

When he pulled up outside of Selena's apartment, he grimaced at the ugly writing on the exterior of the apartment building. Tomorrow, he'd get after it with paint and a scrub brush and wash away the horrible words. With a deep breath, he gathered the flowers, stepped down from his truck, and climbed the stairs to the garage apartment and knocked on the door.

After a long pause, he knocked again. This time, the door opened, and Selena stood before him in yoga pants and a T-shirt, barefooted and clearly not intending to go through with the date. Forcing a smile to his face, he held out the flowers. "These lovely flowers are for a lovely lady. I have a few minutes to wait if you want to get dressed for our date."

She shook her head. "I'm not going."

"Of course, you're going," he said, with all the confidence he could muster. "Everybody in Hellfire will be expecting us to show up somewhere to prove you had the one with the winning bid."

She shook her head. "It was your money. You don't have to prove anything to anyone. And you don't have to take me out on a date."

He nodded, still holding out the flowers in front of him. "I know I don't have to prove anything to anyone. But, I would like to take you out on that date to thank you for saving me from a fate worse than death."

"Perhaps a date with Mrs. Cleyburne would have been preferable to a date with Selena Sanchez."

Forcing his smile a little wider, he held the flowers out again. "I don't suppose you have a vase I could put these flowers in before they start wilting. I saw these as I passed the flower shop, and I thought of you. I know how you like flowers that are cheerful."

Finally, Selena took the flowers from him and walked to the kitchen where she found a vase in the cabinet, filled it with water and put the flowers in it. "Look, Rider," Selena said, "you don't have to take me out on a date. You don't have to take me anywhere. What happened last night was nothing more than a fling. I get that."

Rider waited until she stopped arranging the flowers then he gripped her arms and turned her to face him. "I'm betting you showed up at the garage about the time my ex-wife was trying to convince me to take her back."

Selena looked away. "What you do on your own time, in your garage, with your wife or ex-wife, means nothing to me."

"Well, it means something to me," Rider said. "Lydia did come by my shop today, uninvited. Apparently, she wants me back. Probably because her father cut her off and wants her to go to work to earn her money. I told her I wanted nothing to do with her, him or Dallas, and that our divorce was final. Period. The end."

Selena still refused to meet his gaze. "Seeing you with her reminded me of the difference between you and me."

"What difference?" Rider asked.

She drew in a breath and let it out slowly. "I'm not the kind of woman you need in your life."

"And what kind of woman do I need?" Rider asked.

"I don't know." She flung her hand out to the side. "The beautiful blonde, well put-together, could have been a model... I could never be that. I'm just me, Selena Sanchez. Hispanic, dark haired, dark eyed... someone who doesn't belong in your world."

With his hands still on her arms, Rider gently shook her. "I don't know where you get off thinking you're inferior to me. If anything, you're a better person than I could ever begin to be."

Selena shook her head. "I wasn't born with a silver spoon in my mouth. I didn't go to cotillion when I was a young girl and learn how to set the table correctly with the right number of forks and knives. Hell, I barely know how to set a formal table. I'm not one of the upper class. And I never will be."

"Selena Sanchez, I can't believe you're such a snob." Rider shook his head, a slight smile curving his lips. "If I had said anything like what you just said, you'd have accused me of being an elitist."

Selena stared up into his eyes. "I'm not a snob. I'm just stating the facts."

Gently, Rider ran his hands down her arms. "Fine, prove to me you're not a snob. Go out on this date and show the town of Hellfire you'll go out with someone like me."

"I don't see how that would prove anything," Selena said.

"If nothing else, it'll prove to the Shanes and Rauls, and the ex-wives of the world, that a guy like me *would* go out with a girl like you." He tipped back his head and stared down his nose at her. "Or are you afraid?"

Selena's brow furrowed. "I'm not afraid."

He turned her around and gave her a slight push toward her closet. "Then get dressed. We're going out."

"But I didn't say I'd go out with you," she muttered.

"You have to, now." He didn't give her a chance to change her mind. "I'll step outside while you get dressed. And wear something sexy."

"Why?"

"In case we run into Shane, Raul, or my ex-wife while we're out. I think tonight we should go to the Ugly Stick Saloon."

"Why?" She parroted.

"To kill two birds with one stone. One, that we live up to our promise from the cowboy auction and go on that date that you won. And two, that we prove to everyone that Selena Sanchez could just as easily go out with Rider Grayson as anyone else in Hellfire." He crossed his arms over his chest and gave her a stern look. "Now, are you going to change clothes or are you going to go like you are?"

"I have a mind to go just as I am." Selena tipped her chin upward.

"As you wish." Rider held out his arm. "Let's go."

Selena hesitated. "Well, maybe I'll change into something a little less informal."

He bit back a smile. "I'll be waiting on the landing outside. You've got five minutes."

"I'll be ready in three." Selena turned way and dove for her closet.

Rider chuckled and stepped outside her apartment door, closing it behind him.

Exactly three minutes later, Selena stepped outside the apartment wearing a go-to-hell red dress, strappy silver stilettos, and had her hair pulled up in a loose messy bun that looked so sexy Rider almost turned her around and marched her back into her apartment to make mad, crazy love to her.

She hooked her arm in his and looked up at him. "The Ugly Stick Saloon. One dance. And then you bring me home."

He nodded. "Agreed."

Hope bloomed in Rider's chest as he walked down the stairs with Selena on his arm. He'd gotten her dressed and out the door. Now, all he had to do was take it from there and make it a night she wouldn't forget. One she didn't want to end.

SELENA SAT with her hands primly clasped in her lap as Rider drove away from her apartment. When he'd shown up at her door, she'd convinced herself, again, that she would not go out with him. Seeing his ex-wife in his arms, kissing him like there was no tomorrow, had made her remember everything her father had ever told her as she'd grown up. She was the foreman's daughter. The foreman's family was not a part of the Grayson family, and therefore, she should keep that separation of stations in mind. Always.

Lydia Grayson had driven that lesson home to her. The woman had been so well put together, wearing a tailored suit that was probably handmade just for her, with her hair perfectly coiffed and shoes that probably cost more than three months of Selena's hard-earned salary. While Lydia Grayson dropped a grand on a pair of shoes, Selena scraped and saved so she'd be able to live while she went to PA school. A thousand dollars would pay her rent and utilities, put gas in her car and groceries on her table for a month.

Despite agreeing to just one dance, she didn't demur when Rider treated her to a meal at a local diner, where they ate steak, baked potatoes and a delicious salad. When they finished their meal, they drove to the Ugly Stick Saloon.

The parking lot was full of vehicles, and the music from inside was booming loud enough to shake the tin walls.

Rider found a parking space at the back of the building, pulled in and switched off the engine. Turning to Selena, he asked, "Are you ready?"

Selena shook her head. "I don't know. There are a lot of people inside."

Rider grinned. "All the more reason to make our appearance, have our dance, and then we can leave."

Selena nodded, her jaw firming. She squared her shoulders and glanced at Rider. As small a town as Hellfire was, Selena didn't know what kind of repercussions they'd have by showing up at the Ugly Stick Saloon together on a date. Granted, the date had been "won" at the cowboy auction. Still, when the date was over, and Rider didn't call her again, she didn't want to be seen as a pathetic cast-off of one of the infamous Grayson brothers.

"I'm ready," she said. It was a lie, but she could get through it. As it was, she was leaving in January to go to PA school. Whether or not he ever called her again didn't matter.

As they stepped inside, Audrey Anderson greeted them at the door, smiling broadly. "I'm so glad to see you two here tonight. We have a very special treat in store for you. Everybody in the Ugly Stick Saloon is getting Salsa lessons, and we're Salsa dancing tonight."

"I've never known the Ugly Stick Saloon to have Salsa dancing lessons," Selena mentioned.

Audrey Anderson's smile broadened. "Well, the people spoke! I ran a poll and asked our patrons what kind of dance lessons or what kind of dancing music they'd like to have. One of the top selections was Salsa."

Selena glanced up at Rider. "We don't have to stay if you don't want to," she said.

Rider shrugged. "I'm game if you are."

Her brow furrowed as she stared up at him. "Have you ever danced the Salsa?"

"Maybe." Rider grinned when she raised her brows. "There's a lot you don't know about me." He hooked her arm and urged her into the building.

Selena had grown up with Latino music. At any

family reunion, they could be guaranteed the music would be loud, laughter would be plentiful, and Salsa was as natural as breathing and eating tamales. She had no doubt she could do the Salsa. But Rider?

Rider claimed a small table and ordered drinks for himself and Selena.

Meanwhile, Audrey took the stage with a microphone and quieted the music. "Tonight's a special night," she said. "Tonight, we're having our first Salsa dancing lesson. Is everybody ready?" A loud cheer arose from the patrons of the Ugly Stick Saloon. "Here to give you a good example of what Salsa looks like, is Raul Jemenez and Marisol Perez." Music started, and Raul and Marisol appeared on the stage doing a Salsa to the beat of the sexy music.

Selena smiled. "I didn't know Raul could dance."

"How long did you two date?" Rider asked. "You don't have to answer, if you don't want to."

Selena shrugged. "Only a few weeks. We didn't do much; we just went out to dinner a couple times. We didn't find much to talk about."

Audrey took the mic again and announced, "Anyone who wants to learn the steps, please join us on the dance floor."

Several women grabbed the hands of their men and dragged them out on the dance floor.

Rider held out his hand to Selena. "Ready to give it a try?"

Selena frowned and put her hand in his, a little

hesitant. "Does this count as our one and only dance?"

"If one is all you want," Rider said. "But you're welcome to claim more than one dance."

Selena rose from her chair and followed Rider onto the wooden dance floor. He held one of her hands up and rested his other hand on her hip. Moments later, he was leading her in a snappy Salsa, his hips moving to the rhythm of the music, as if he'd been born to do it.

Selena laughed, "Where did you learn to Salsa?"

"A good friend I met in college, also a Mexican National, taught me how. She was quite a good dancer. She married my roommate. They already have two small children. I'm their godfather." He spun her around and dipped her low.

Selena couldn't remember having such a good dance partner, and she enjoyed every minute of the Salsa. One dance led into another, until finally the music slowed into a very sensuous, Latino slow dance. Rider gathered her close in his arms as they moved and swayed to the music. She leaned into the hard muscles of his chest and rested her cheek in the crook of his neck. The more they swayed together, the more she wished they were alone somewhere else. She wanted to feel his hands on her naked body as they had been the night before. Eventually, the music slowed to a stop, and a new beat started up, fast and furious. Selena didn't feel like doing the

Salsa anymore. She wanted to leave and be alone with Rider.

He tipped up her chin. "Are you ready to go?"

She nodded, more than ready to leave. She was ready to have him all to herself.

As he led her off the dance floor, she glanced around the room. There at a table, close to the exit door, sat a blonde-haired woman in a black cocktail-length dress. Her hair was pulled up, her makeup perfectly applied. It was Lydia. Rider's ex-wife. And she was sitting with Shane Fetterlein. Selena glanced up at Rider.

His gaze moved to his ex-wife, and he frowned. "What the hell is she doing here?"

Selena didn't respond. She ducked her head and moved toward the door. "If you want to stay here, you can. But I'm ready to leave."

Rider shook his head. "Oh, I don't want to stay here at all. I have other plans." He gathered her close with an arm around her waist and led her out the door.

Once outside, Selena turned to Rider. "Seriously, if you want to stay and make sure your ex-wife is okay, I'll understand."

Rider shook his head. "I have no desire to stick around and see what my ex is up to. I just don't like the idea of her and Shane putting their heads together and cooking up something."

"It can only mean trouble," Selena agreed.

He took her hand in his and lead her toward the truck. "But, if you're not too tired, I have something else in mind. Are you game?"

Selena thought back to his ex-wife sitting in the Ugly Stick Saloon. Rider had chosen to stay with her rather than go back to Lydia. Her heart swelled with hope. "I'm game," she said.

"Good. I have something special planned."

He helped her up into the truck and took off, not toward her apartment, but in the direction of the open countryside. Before long, they came to a bluff, a place where young couples came to neck and make out.

Selena's body heated at the thought.

Rider pulled the truck to a stop overlooking a valley below. Above them, the stars spread out like a blanket of diamonds in the sky. He got out, reached into the back seat, pulled out a sleeping bag and tossed it onto the truck's bed. Next, he unearthed a basket and laid it in the back of the truck, as well.

Then he held his hand out to Selena. "Would you care to join me and do a bit of stargazing?"

Selena put her hand in his. "I'd love to."

He helped her up into the back of the truck. Together, they spread out the sleeping bag and laid on top of it, looking up at the stars.

Rider leaned up on his elbow and pulled a bottle of wine from the basket, along with two wine glasses. "I got your favorite, Cabernet Sauvignon."

Selena tilted her head. "How did you know?"

"I asked Audrey what you ordered at the auction."

Selena smiled. He'd gone to a lot of trouble to get it right. She sat, took the glass he poured and sipped from it, her gaze on the stars above, but keeping Rider in her peripheral vision.

"I thought you might enjoy this, since the meteor shower is supposed to be at its peak tonight. We don't have to do anything but watch the stars, with nobody to bother us."

They touched their glasses together.

Rider toasted, "To starry skies and good friends."

Selena added, "And to learning more about each other."

They sipped their wine, the stress of the day melting from Selena's shoulders. Soon, the wine, the stars above and the handsome man beside her lulled her into a sense of serenity, and more than that. She set her empty glass aside and reclined. She stared up at the stars as, one by one, the meteors streaked across the sky.

Rider reached for her hand and held it inside his.

Selena wanted more than him holding her hand. She turned on her side and stared across at him. "What is it you want from life, Rider?"

Rider cupped her cheek. "Right at this minute, all I want is to kiss you."

Selena made that wish come true. She lowered

her face and touched her lips to his. Her kiss was gentle, exploring his mouth, taking her time.

But a few moments later, he flipped her on her back and crushed her lips with his, his tongue diving inside her mouth to give hers a possessive caress. When he raised his head for air, he glanced down into her eyes. "I need you to know that the kiss you witnessed earlier, between my ex and myself, was all initiated by her. I never kissed her back. I would never kiss her knowing how much I enjoy kissing you." Again, he lowered his mouth to hers and took her in a gentle kiss that slowly became much more. His hands roamed over her body and slipped beneath the hem of her dress.

Selena tugged the shirt from his waistband and ran her hands up his torso to the hard planes of his chest.

Soon, the need to feel flesh against flesh had them tearing at each other's clothes, removing them and tossing them to the side. Before long, they were naked in the back of his truck, making love.

They could have been there minutes or hours. Selena didn't know. She didn't care. She just knew she was happy to be in his arms. When at last they lay side by side, satiated, and once again staring up at the stars, she sighed. "I'm not changing my mind."

"I don't expect you to," he responded. "I know you're going to school in January. But I'll be here when you get back. In fact, if you want me to, I'll come visit while you're gone. I own my own business. I can come and go as I please."

"I don't want you making any promises you won't keep," Selena said, even as her heart soared at his suggestion.

"Trust me, I won't make any promises I don't intend to keep."

Selena sighed and pressed her naked body close to his. "I don't know what tomorrow will bring, but tonight couldn't be more perfect." She wished it could go on forever.

CHAPTER 10

RIDER FLUNG the eighty-pound hay bale up on the back of the trailer and wiped the sweat from his brow.

"Thanks for coming out to haul hay with us today," his brother Beckett said.

"Yeah, I wanted to say thanks, too," Big John Grayson said as he stepped down from the pickup truck. "Takes all of us men to haul in enough hay to feed the cattle through the dry spells and the winter."

"Hey, don't forget about me," Lily said from the top of the stack. She was sweating just as much as the men, and her hair had strands of straw poking out of it.

Chance chuckled. "That's right. Don't forget our little sis."

"She's as much help as any one of you men," Nash

said and tossed another bale up to the top of the stack.

Lily positioned it neatly and waited for the next one.

"I'm surprised you're out this early," Chance said to Rider. "After spending the evening dancing at the Ugly Stick Saloon, I'm surprised you have enough energy left to even lift a bale of hay."

"Was that your cowboy auction date?" Lily asked from the top of the pile.

Rider hefted another bale and tossed it up to where Lily was at the top before answering. "Officially, yes. That was my date with Selena for bidding on me at the auction."

"Where did she get seven thousand dollars to purchase a date with a cowboy?" Nash asked.

"It wasn't her money," Chance said. "Rider made that donation and had Selena do the bidding to save him from any potential disaster dates."

"So, you really didn't have to take Selena out on a date, did you?" Lily asked.

Rider shrugged. "I felt it was the least I could do, after she put forth the effort to bid on me."

Lily stood at the top of the hay stack hands perched on her hips. "Really? It was nothing more than just an obligation?"

Heat rose up Rider's neck and into his cheeks. "Well, it might have been a little more than that."

Lily grinned. "I'm glad to see you finally noticed that our Selena is a full-grown woman now."

"Who said she wasn't?" Chance said. "We all had to grow up sometime."

"Well, it took some of us a little longer to notice." Lily cocked her eyebrows and stared at her brother Rider. "Am I right? You finally noticed that Selena is a grown woman? What I want to know now is what are your intentions toward her?"

"I'd like to know the answer to that as well," Pedro Sanchez said as he joined them. He'd been manning the tractor, baling the hay as they had been picking up the hay bales and loading them onto the trailer. Pedro had finished his line of hay baling and had come to join them to stack the bales on the trailer. "What are your intentions toward my daughter?"

Everyone paused in what they were doing and waited for Rider's answer. He felt as if they had all ganged up on him. But the one person whose desire to learn the truth mattered most was the one person he did not want to offend.

"I do not want my daughter hurt," Mr. Sanchez said.

"Mr. Sanchez," Rider started. "I have no intention of hurting your daughter. I want only the best for her."

"My daughter is scheduled to start school in January. I hope you don't intend to get in the way of her accomplishing her educational goals."

"Mr. Sanchez," Rider said. "I want what your daughter wants. Selena means a lot to me. I would never do anything to hurt her, or to get in the way of her accomplishing her dreams."

"Then what is it you want with my daughter?" Pedro Sanchez asked.

"Yeah, Rider," Big John Grayson crossed his arms over his chest, "Selena is a good girl. I won't have one of my sons mucking up her life."

"Dad, Mr. Sanchez," Rider said, "I think I might be in love with Selena." There, he'd said it.

A collective gasp rose from all parties witnessing Rider's declaration.

Big John shook his head. "Son, you're fresh out of a bad marriage. Have you considered she might be your rebound from your divorce?"

Rider looked around at all the faces staring back at him and nodded. "I have considered that. My marriage had ended long before we signed the papers. I didn't realize, until I came back to Hellfire all I'd been missing. Yes, I missed my family and friends. But it was more than that. And when I saw Selena...everything seemed to fall into place. What I knew about Selena, was the same, but different. I mean hell, we grew up together. We rode horses together. We like so many of the same things. I think I've always loved Selena. But now it's different." He shook his head. "I'm not explaining this very well. Shoot, I'm not even sure how it happened."

"Please, Mr. Grayson," Pedro said. "Don't break my daughter's heart. She does not belong in your world. In the world with the Graysons."

Rider frowned. "How can you say that?" He turned and paced the length of the trailer, spun and came back. "Selena grew up with us. She hung out with us, she helped haul hay, she did everything we did. How does she not fit in with our world?"

"Yeah," Lily said, "what do you mean she doesn't fit in our world? She's like a sister to me."

"And to me," Chance said.

"And me," Nash and Beckett said at the same time.

Big John Grayson slipped an arm over Pedro's shoulder. "Pedro, my old friend, ya have to admit it. You're more family than employee."

Pedro shook his head. "We will always be your employees. Me and my wife Margarita."

Big John dropped his arm from around Pedro and stared at the man, a frown making deep grooves in his forehead. "Do I have to fire you to prove that we are like family?"

Pedro's lips quirked as he shook his head. "I don't want to be fired."

"How can you say we're not like family when we spend most of our days together? My Ann and your Margarita go to the same quilting bee. They belong to the same garden club. You and I have had beers together at the Ugly Stick Saloon. How is it you think that we are not like family?"

Pedro shook his head. "We are Hispanic. You are white. In many people's thoughts and minds, the two races do not mix."

Rider shook his head. "Not to us. We're all one big family. It doesn't matter the color of our skin or the nature of our origins. So what if your family is all from Mexico. Mine were from who knows where? Scotland, Wales, England, Africa maybe. Who knows where? Maybe Ireland. Maybe Romania. We're all pretty much the same, everything mixed in together. It doesn't matter. What matters is love. Who do you love? Pedro, you and Margarita are like family to me. You're like my second father and mother. We love you guys as much as we love Mom and Dad."

Big John nodded. "What my son is saying is true, Pedro. This business of eating in the kitchen while the Grayson family eats at the formal dining table is over. We will all eat together, or we won't eat at all."

"Amen," said Lily.

Pedro nodded. "I appreciate what you're saying. But what happens when Rider decides he no longer loves Selena? Everything will get awkward at that point. He will break my daughter's heart. I will find that difficult to forgive, and I will not feel the same way toward a boy who once was like a son to me." Pedro faced Rider. "Can you guarantee that you won't break my daughter's heart? That you will always be there for her?"

Rider sighed. "I don't know where everything is

going between me and Selena. All I know is I want it to continue going."

"My daughter leaves in January, and she won't be back for two years during her training. Are you telling me that you will wait for her?"

Rider nodded. "I'm willing to wait for Selena. She's everything I could ever want in a woman. I realize that now, after my divorce, that I don't know what got in my head when I married to begin with. I think I was trying to fit into a place that I didn't belong. I don't belong in Dallas. Hellfire is my home. It's where I want to be. It's where I've always wanted to be. Because of the people who live here."

"And if my daughter doesn't want to stay in Hellfire?" Pedro asked.

Rider pressed a hand to his heart. "I will take her wishes into consideration. I only want to make her happy. If leaving Hellfire will make her happy, I will go with her. I would hope that someday she would want to return to Hellfire. It, too, is her home."

Big John nodded. "I understand your concern for your daughter, but like all families we'll work through whatever happens."

The old time CB radio inside Big John's truck squawked. Big John's brow furrowed. "I wonder what that's all about. I haven't heard that thing go off in so long I can't remember." He climbed into the truck, lifted the mic and spoke with whoever was on the other end. When he came back out he nodded towards his sons. "That was a call from dispatch. All volunteer firefighters are asked to report in. They have a grass fire closing in on the edge of Hellfire. It's getting close to the trailer park out on the south side of town. They want everybody who can help to come out."

"Guess that means us," Chance said. Of the four brothers, he was the only fulltime firefighter.

"Aren't you off duty?" Nash asked.

"If they're asking for all hands, I guess they might not care if I'm a volunteer or a full-timer," he said. "I'm in."

"You boys go," Big John said. "Lily, Pedro, and I will get this load of hay to the barnyard. Then we'll join you, if you still need our help."

The four Rider sons ran for Nash's truck parked on the edge of the hayfield and climbed into the cab.

"Must be pretty bad if they're asking all volunteers to report," Chance said.

All four men fell silent as they sped toward town. As they got closer they could see smoke billowing up along a line on the southern edge of town. A lot of people lived on the south side. People who couldn't afford to rebuild their lives, who lived on the edge from paycheck to paycheck.

When they reached town, they swung by the fire department and collected protective clothing and equipment. They didn't take long, and were back on the road and headed south as soon as possible.

Volunteer firefighters had parked their trucks and cars along the sides of the road headed south out of town and walked in from there. It wasn't long before Rider, Nash, Beckett, and Chance found the fire chief and received their orders of where they should begin and what they should try to save first.

"The fire line stretches all the way from Joe Sarley's farm all the way to the highway. The smoke is getting so bad that its affecting traffic. We're not allowing cars to pass through on the highway. We have the sheriff's department stationed on the highway to turn people away on either side," the fire chief said. "Our one pumper truck belonging to the county has been filled twice and has sprayed water along the edges, but it doesn't seem to be helping and the wind is picking up. We have two more pumper trucks coming in from surrounding counties. We've commandeered every track loader and bulldozer we could from construction sites, farms and ranches around and they're headed this way to help with the beak line. We need every man on deck to put out fires and to tamp down any new ones that spring up from the embers."

The Grayson brothers knew the drill. They'd been through this several times before. Grabbing rakes, axes, and wet burlap sacks, they went to work.

JUST AFTER ONE O'CLOCK, Selena clocked out at the

convenience store and waved goodbye to Mr. Hutcheson. "I'll see you tomorrow morning," she called out.

"Study hard, girl. We're expecting a lot from our hometown gal," Mr. Hutcheson called back.

Selena had all intentions of going home, cracking the books and spending the rest of her evening absorbing as much information as possible. She'd put off studying for her test for far too long.

As she walked toward her apartment, all she could think about was the night before. Staring up at the stars, holding hands, kissing and making love with Rider Grayson.

As she passed his garage she decided to stop in and say hello. Perhaps he wasn't too busy, and he wouldn't mind a visitor. Maybe he would share the cookies that she had left the day before. Hell, she just wanted to see his face and hear his voice. Any excuse was good enough for her.

When she paused in front of Rider's garage, she wondered why the overhead door was closed. She tried the smaller door to his office. It was locked. It wasn't like Rider to close up shop on a weekday.

Selena went around to the side and climbed the stairs to the apartment above the garage. She chuckled thinking how much their circumstances were alike. They both lived in small apartments over garages. They both liked staring up at the stars and watching the meteor showers. And they both liked making love with nothing but stars and skies overhead. She really hoped that she would find him at home and that they could pick up where they left off the night before.

When she arrived at the top of the stairs she noticed the door was slightly ajar. She pushed it open and stepped inside. "Rider?" She stared around the room noticing how papers were strewn across the room. Drawers were emptied, dumped onto the floor, and the cushions had been ripped off the couch and flung aside.

What the hell? "Rider? Are you all right?" She picked her way through the mess, searching for the man who'd captured her heart, praying that he hadn't passed out on the floor or was injured or had a heart attack. Hell, she didn't know what had happened. But the place was a disaster.

Behind her the door shut with a sharp click. Selena spun to face a blonde-haired intruder in a designer royal blue dress.

"Lydia," Selena said, "what are you doing here?"

Rider's ex-wife twisted the dead bolt lock on the door and tipped her chin upward. "I'm Rider's wife. I'm here to collect my man."

Selena glanced around the room. "Are you the one who did this to Rider's home?"

She laughed. "You call this a home? It's a hovel. We had a beautiful seven thousand square foot home in the best part of Dallas. And he left it to come to this filthy, stinking, disgrace of a garage. To live in a tiny apartment even my maid wouldn't consider appropriate. Rider is a fool to believe that this is where he belongs."

"Rider is not the fool," Selena said, "you are. This is what Rider wants. He wants to work with his hands. He likes making things work and figuring things out. And he doesn't like living in a big city where there is too much traffic and too many people. He likes being out in the open air, in the country side."

"Rider doesn't know what he wants," Lydia said. "He needs to be where he can make the most of his life. Where he can make the most money. Where he can be the most influential. And that's working with my father's firm."

Selena snorted. "You mean Rider needs to be where he can be making money to support you, am I right?"

"Yes," Lydia said. "We were married. He promised for better or for worse to support me. To be there forever and ever, amen!"

Selena shook her head. "That's not how it works sweetheart. Marriage is a partnership. People involved should understand the other's likes, needs and wants. And there should be compromise on both sides. And they should pool together their resources to make a life together."

"Blah, blah, blah," Lydia said, "How am I supposed to survive without a husband to support me?"

Selena couldn't believe what she was hearing. "Are you serious? Is that the only reason you want Rider back? To pay for your expensive shoes and designer clothes?"

"What do you know about the life I lead in Dallas? There are expectations of everything I do. I'm always in the public eye. I'm expected to act a certain way, and dress a certain way and be at all the right places with all the right people."

Selena snorted. "And Rider was your means to an end."

"Yes, dammit. He promised to love, honor, and cherish me. And to support me through thick and thin. Well, he's not doing his job."

"From what I understand, you didn't do your job. It was in all the tabloids that you cheated on him."

She shrugged. "He was never home. What was I supposed to do? I was lonely."

Selena shook her head. The woman really didn't have a clue. "You were supposed to be faithful. To honor your commitment to him. Maybe he wouldn't have worked so many long hours if he hadn't had to earn so much money to support you and your expensive lifestyle."

"What do you know...you...you...tramp." Lydia gritted her teeth and screamed, "Maybe he would come back to me and Dallas if you hadn't tempted him to stay!" She rushed toward Selena and shoved her hard.

Selena stumbled backward, fell, and hit her head against the corner of a cabinet. She hadn't been prepared for an attack. She never would have guessed that Lydia had it in her to be physically violent. Those few thoughts flitted through her mind as darkness blurred her vision. Thoughts spun through her mind, but her head swam in the haze, dragging her under.

As she struggled to stay awake, she heard Lydia say, "If this place isn't here, and if you aren't here, he'll come back to me. Just you watch." She laughed. "Oh wait, you won't be here to watch."

Like a light being dimmed, Selena's consciousness faded to black.

CHAPTER 11

AN HOUR into fighting the grass fire that edged closer to the south side of town, Rider glanced up long enough to notice that just about everybody from Hellfire had come out to pitch in and stop the fire's spread.

At one point, he came across Raul and Shane working side by side, slapping at the embers and stomping on the startup fires. They worked in quiet concentration, respectful of each other's efforts to stop the destruction.

And they did stop the destruction.

A hundred yards from the most outlying house in Hellfire, firefighters brought the grass fire to a halt. The winds died down, and a cheer went up from all the people covered in soot as they stomped on the last ember and doused the final flame.

Rider glanced up, looking for his brothers. Nash

155

and Beckett were close at hand, but Chance had disappeared. He gathered close to his brothers. "Anybody seen Chance?" he asked.

Nash nodded. "He asked for my keys a few minutes ago. He said he'd be right back." As if on cue, Nash's truck raced up to them and spun sideways to a stop. Chance opened the door, stepped out on the running board and yelled out over the top of the truck. "Get in. We have another fire to fight."

Nash and Beckett jumped in the back. Rider slid into the front passenger seat.

"Close the door." Chance shifted into drive and hit the accelerator hard, shooting the truck forward, heading back toward Hellfire. Already, they could see a plume of smoke rising from the middle of town.

"Where's the new fire?" Nash asked.

Chance shot a glance at Rider. "Dispatch says it's at your garage."

"My garage?" Rider shook his head. "I know I didn't leave anything running." He frowned and stared at the rising column of smoke. His pulse beat fast as he leaned forward in his seat.

As they left the brush fire, Rider noted that other firefighters were loading up onto the fire engine, and it turned in a circle to head back toward town. The Grayson brothers would arrive sooner than the fire engine or anybody else. When they passed the convenience store, Mr. Hutcheson was standing outside, staring down the street toward the billowing smoke.

Rider wondered if Selena was working at the store. Would she be worried when she found out that his garage was up in flames?

Rider wasn't as concerned about the things that were in the garage or in the apartment above as much as he was concerned about the fire spreading to other buildings within the town. Fortunately, Selena's apartment was a couple blocks further along than his and should be all right.

He pulled his cellphone from his pocket and dialed Selena's number just to make sure she wasn't anywhere close to the fire. Her line rang five times before her voicemail picked up. She was probably still at work, or maybe in the shower at her apartment.

When they pulled up in front of the garage, flames shot around the base of the building and up the wooden steps to the apartment above. Already, he could see fire climbing the curtains in the upstairs windows. Then a flash of blonde hair and a royal blue dress caught his attention.

"Holy shit!" Nash exclaimed. "Is that Lydia?"

Rider leaped out of the truck before it even came to a full stop. He ran toward the woman who disappeared around the side of the building. When he caught up to her, he found her carrying a jug of gasoline, splashing its contents on the side of his building. He ran after her, yelling, "Lydia, stop!"

She laughed hysterically and flung the jug at him, splashing gasoline across his legs.

"You'll see," she said, "when this place is gone, when *she's* gone, you'll come back to me." She spun and darted away.

Chance raced past Rider and tackled Lydia, crushing her body beneath his on the ground. He pinned her wrists above her head and straddled her hips. "What the hell do you think you're doing?"

"What do you mean, Lydia?" Rider asked as he knelt beside her. "What do you mean by *when this place is gone, and when she's gone?* Who are you talking about?"

Lydia laughed in his face, her eyes wide. "Your girlfriend," she said. "When this place is gone, she'll be gone with it."

"Are you talking about Selena?" Rider demanded. He shoved Chance aside and yanked Lydia to her feet. "Tell me what you're talking about."

Lydia wrapped her arms around Rider's neck. "I told her you'd come back to me. When this place was gone, when she was gone, you'd come back to me."

Rider peeled her arms from around his neck, gripped her shoulders and held her at arm's length. "Where is Selena? When did you talk with her last?"

Lydia smiled. "She came to see you. I just made sure she stayed until you got home." Her eyes narrowed. "You're a fool to think you could fall in love with someone like her. She's not even in the same class as you are."

Rider shook Lydia. "Where is Selena?"

Her grin broadened. "I guess you'll have to find her."

Rider shoved Lydia toward Chance. "Don't let her get away." And he raced towards the steps leading up to his apartment. Only the steps were consumed in flame, the boards charred and falling through the risers. He couldn't go up them. Fire had already eaten through the planks and the railing. He had no way to get to the upstairs apartment.

Chance passed Lydia to Nash. "Cuff her or something. Don't let her get away. She's responsible for this. And she may have hurt Selena. We have a fire to put out." He ran around the side of the garage and found a water hose. The puny hose was the best they could do until the firetruck arrived.

Already Rider could hear the wail of the sirens in the distance, but he was afraid they'd arrive too late to save Selena if she was in the upstairs apartment. Rider ran to his brother Nash. "Give me a boost. Help me reach that upstairs window."

Nash glanced at the window and looked back at Rider. "You'll never reach it."

"I have to. Selena's in my apartment."

Nash's eyes widened. "You can't get up those stairs. They're already destroyed."

ELLE JAMES

"Then I have to get up to a window," Rider said, jabbing a finger toward one of the windows above.

"Can you get inside the garage? Is there a ladder anywhere?" Beckett asked.

A ladder? Yes! Rider thought. "Inside the garage hanging on the wall. If I can get inside the bay, I can get the ladder and climb up to Selena."

Flames fueled by the gasoline climbed the walls of the exterior of the garage. Rider stripped his T-shirt from his back, wrapped his hands in it and ran for the door to the garage. Using the T-shirt, he grabbed the hot knob and twisted it.

The knob wouldn't turn.

He dug in his pocket for his keys, slipped the key in the door, and then using the T-shirt, he twisted the knob. The door opened. He pressed the T-shirt to his nose, ducked low and ran inside the garage. Smoke blackened the walls and filled the air, stinging his lungs as he breathed through the fabric of the shirt. He felt his way along the inside of the garage until he found the ladder hanging on the wall and removed it.

Hunching below the ceiling of smoke, he worked his way toward the overhead door. He laid the ladder on the ground, slid the lever open on the overhead door and raised it above his head. Smoke billowed out. Rider dove through the door, out into the fresh air. He coughed and pointed back toward the ladder he'd left on the floor. "Get the ladder," he said, his voice coming out gravely, the effort to speak painful.

Nash ran in, grabbed the ladder and brought it back out. He extended it as far as it would go and leaned it on the outside of the garage. It came up four feet short of the window above.

Flames rose up all around the ladder. Anybody would be a fool to climb it.

Rider had to if Selena was up there. He had to get to her. Refusing to leave her to die, he started up the ladder, the flames licking at his clothes and the gasoline Lydia had splashed on his legs. Seconds later, his jeans caught fire. Forced to stop, he jumped back to the ground and rolled until the flames were extinguished. Immediately he leapt to his feet and started up the ladder again. Chance grabbed him before he got too far and pulled him back.

"You can't do it." Chance said.

"I have to," Rider said. "Selena's up there."

Chance shoved the water hose into his brother's hands. "Then I'll go up."

Rider shook his head no. "I need to."

Chance started up the ladder. "I'm the one who does this fulltime. I know what I'm doing. You man the water hose until the truck arrives. While you're at it, rinse the accelerant off your legs."

Rider watched as his brother climbed the ladder, flames rising up around him, smoke billowed into the air.

SOMETHING TICKLED SELENA'S THROAT, making her cough. The cough shook her awake, and she blinked her eyes. Some kind of fog hovered above her, and heat built in the air around her. She tried to take a deep breath, but all she got was smoke pulled into her lungs. Again, she coughed and rolled over onto her hands and knees. That was when she remembered she was in Rider's apartment. An apartment filled with smoke, with flames climbing up at the walls. She had to get out.

Still on her hands and knees, she crawled for the door, reached for the handle and tried to turn it. It wouldn't open. She braced her feet against the wall and pulled as hard as she could on the doorknob. Still, the door refused to budge. Crawling back toward one of the windows, she tried to slide the window up, but the paint on the window and the sill was stuck together. She couldn't open the window, and the smoke was getting thicker.

Selena pulled her shirt up over her mouth, but she couldn't stop coughing. Her eyes burned, and her lungs burned. She only had minutes, maybe seconds, before she succumbed to smoke inhalation. If she didn't get out soon, she would die. Hunkering as low as she could to the floor to avoid the smoke, she felt her way around until her fingers closed on the leg of a chair. Hope surged as she climbed to her feet. Dragging the chair along behind her, she moved to where she thought a window was.

Selena rose with the chair in her hands and swung it as hard as she could, hitting the window. Her first swing only cracked the glass. She reared back and swung again. The chair crashed through the window, catching on the jagged shards.

Coughing with every breath, she jerked the chair back and used it to scrape the glass away from the windowsill. Smoke swirled through the opening. She gave it a second or two to clear enough that she could put her head through the window and stare down at the ground.

A few men milled about on the driveway below, mere shadows in the fading light. With her eyes stinging, she could barely make out who they were. Someone had put a ladder up against the window on the other side of the room. A man was climbed up amid the flames. She recognized him as Chance Grayson.

Someone called out from the ground. "Selena."

Selena glanced down at the man whose familiar voice made her heart swell with hope. "Rider," she tried to say, her voice coming out no more than a croak. And she coughed. After she coughed, she inhaled, sucking more smoke into her lungs.

An explosion below shook the building. Selena gripped the window frame. Pain shot through her as her hands were sliced by jagged edges of glass.

"Jump, Selena," Rider urged. "You have to get out of the building, now."

Glancing around her, she pulled an afghan from a nearby chair and placed it over the edge of the window. Then she slung her leg over the window sill, turned over on her stomach and eased herself out through the broken pane. She lowered herself until only her hands were holding onto the windowsill, her feet dangling in the air.

"Let go, Selena," Rider said. "I'll catch you."

She couldn't tell where he was. All she could do was go on faith and pray she didn't hurt him in the fall.

"Let go, Selena," Rider urged. "It'll be okay. I'll catch you."

With smoke and flames rising up around her, Selena released her hold on the windowsill and dropped through the air. As she neared the ground, arms grabbed hold of her, breaking her fall. But she came down so hard that Rider's legs crumpled beneath him, and they both ended up on the ground.

He scrambled from beneath her, lifted her and carried her away from the burning building. When they were well out of danger, he laid her out on the ground and pushed sooty hair out of her face.

"Are you okay?" he asked.

She coughed, nodded, and coughed again. She couldn't seem to clear the soot from her lungs.

By that time, the fire engine had arrived, the lights strobing in the evening dusk. An ambulance pulled up on the street, and emergency medical technicians jumped out, grabbed a medical kit and converged on her. In the next few seconds, she was fitted with an oxygen mask, transferred to a stretcher and loaded into the back of the ambulance. She held out her hand and coughed. "Rider," she called out.

Rider appeared at her side. He climbed into the ambulance with her, and together they rode off to a nearby hospital.

Selena blinked her eyes, trying to clear the smoke from them so that she could stare up at the most wonderful man she could have ever imagined. And he was holding her hand and saying soothing words to her she didn't understand, nor did she care. They just sounded good. She held on tight to his fingers, afraid to let go, afraid that if she closed her eyes, he would disappear. Despite all her effort to keep her eyes open, they drifted closed.

At the hospital, they wheeled her back into an examination room. When they asked Rider if he was a family member, he nodded and said, "Yes, I'm her fiancé." They allowed him to come back with her, without asking for proof. Selena didn't care what he told them, as long as he remained with her.

The doctor examined her and declared she had a case of smoke inhalation, insisting she remain overnight for observation. They also wanted to get Rider on oxygen and keep him as well, but he insisted he was fine and that he would stay with Selena through the night.

They moved Selena to a private room where Rider sat in a chair beside her. She fell asleep with him holding her hand. When she woke later that evening, others had arrived in her room, including her father, her mother, Big John Grayson, and all the Grayson brothers and Lily.

She laughed and coughed. "How did they let you all in?"

Everyone smiled. Big John had the biggest grin, answering, "We told them we were family. They didn't ask questions; they just let us come in."

Selena glanced up at her father. "Papa?"

He took her hand in his, and he brought it up to his face. "Yes, *mi hija*."

"Don't worry about me," she said. "I'm going to be all right."

Her father shook his head. "I will always worry about you, *mi corazón*."

Her mother moved up beside her and brushed her sooty hair from her forehead. "We will always worry about you," she said, and she glanced around at all the Graysons crowded into the room. "We are *familia*," she said. "We will always worry about the people we love."

Big John Grayson slipped an arm around his wife's waist. "Come on, gang, let's give her some air. She looks like she can use some. We love you, Selena. Get well soon."

Her father bent and pressed his lips to her forehead. "I love you, *mi hija*," he said.

Her mama kissed her as well. "We'll be close by," she promised.

The room cleared out of everyone except Rider, who sat beside her in a soot-covered tee and jeans.

She looked at him and gave him half a smile. "You don't have to stay."

He shook his head. "Yes, I do." He lifted her hand to his lips and pressed a kiss to her knuckles.

She liked the feeling of his lips on her skin. "I'm going to be all right," she said. "You don't have to worry about me."

He shook his head. "Yes, I do," he repeated. "When I saw you in the window with the smoke and the fire all around you, all I could think was I don't want to live without you. I can't. Babe, you're my heart, my soul. You're everything I've dreamed of, the missing piece that makes my life complete. When you let go of the windowsill, I thought I'd lose you. That split second that you fell, everything became crystal clear to me. You're the person I want to spend my life with. You're the one I love."

Selena's heart swelled. Her eyes filled with tears. "What about Lydia?"

His hand squeezed hers, and his jaw tightened. "Lydia is in jail. She's been charged with attempted murder. I'm sure her father will have her out in no time. But as far as I'm concerned, she can rot in hell for what she tried to do to you."

Selena's lips curled into a gentle smile. "I almost feel sorry for her."

Rider stared down at her, a frown pulling his eyebrows together. "The woman tried to kill you, and you feel sorry for her?"

Selena nodded, "Yes. Somewhere along the line, someone should have told her no, and they didn't. I have a feeling she went through life getting everything she wanted, and then when she couldn't have you, she didn't know how to respond."

"You're much more generous to her than I'd be. When I found out she'd tried to kill you, I was ready to kill her myself. And I might have, but I had to get you out of that burning apartment first."

Selena lifted his hand to her cheek and pressed her lips to it. "Thank you for catching me when I fell."

"Thank you for trusting me to catch you." He bent and pressed his lips to hers in a gentle kiss.

Selena wrapped her arms around the back of his neck and pulled him close, deepening the kiss. But when a cough shook her, he backed away and gave her the space she needed.

She chuckled and coughed again. "Sorry about that."

He tucked a strand of her hair behind her ear. "Sweetheart, I'm just glad to hear you coughing. It means you're alive."

She scooted over on the bed and patted the sheet beside her. "Come here," she said.

He climbed up on the bed, laid down beside her and gathered her in his arms.

She snuggled against him, pressing her cheek against his chest where she could hear the strong, steady beat of his heart. "Tell me what just happened with my parents and with all the Graysons crowded into one room at the same time."

"The Sanchezes and the Graysons came to an understanding. I think we all realized that we're just one big family, and that we should always treat each other as if we are brothers, sisters, and whatever. Lily and my brothers think of you as their sister," Rider said.

Selena smiled. "And you?"

Rider's lips spread into a wide grin. "Sweetheart, I don't think of you as a sister." He nuzzled her neck. "Nope. Not a sister."

Selena chuckled and coughed. "Good thing. Because I don't think of you as a brother. I certainly wouldn't kiss a brother like I want to kiss you." She lifted her face to accept his lips on hers.

EPILOGUE

ONE MONTH LATER.

"I have the steaks," Rider called out as he pushed through screen door out onto the back patio where the Graysons and the Sanchezes had gathered to celebrate. "Grab the chicken and the barbecue sauce, and we're good."

"How is it that we're celebrating your engagement to Selena, but you and Selena are doing all the cooking?" Nash sat in a lounge chair with his fiancée Phoebe beside him.

"At the rate they're going, Rider and Selena will be married before you and me," Phoebe said.

"I told you I was willing to fly to Vegas and make an honest woman of you, pronto," Nash teased.

"I wouldn't dream of depriving you of wedding day jitters, wearing a tuxedo and standing in front of every resident of Hellfire, Texas to pledge your love and say your *I do*'s to me." Phoebe patted his hand. "Two more months, sweetheart. You'll have to wait."

Nash lifted Phoebe's hand to his lips and kissed her knuckles. "It'll be well worth it. I can't wait to spend the rest of my life with you."

"And I with you." Phoebe stared into Nash's eyes, her love practically glowing in her cheeks.

Rider grinned, happy to see his brother so much in love. A month ago, he would've cringed at all the mushy talk, but now that Selena had promised to marry him, he found himself feeling just as love-struck.

Two men walked around the back of the house enjoying the party on the patio.

"Shane, Raul, I'm glad you two could make it," Rider said.

Shane gave Rider a chin lift and a wave. "We appreciate the invite."

Raul nodded. "Besides, the fish were biting at the lake." He winked.

Rider chuckled. "Nice to know our little party won out over a fishing trip."

Selena stepped onto the porch carrying a tray full of raw chicken and a bottle of barbecue sauce. She smiled at Shane and Raul. "Oh good, you made it after all."

Rider took the tray from her hands and laid it

beside the grill. Then he turned to the two men and cleared his throat. "Selena and I wanted to thank you two personally for bringing us together."

Shane frowned. "How did we do that?"

"If you two hadn't gotten into that fight in front of the convenience store that day, Rider and I might not be together now." Selena smiled up at Rider. "Thank you for being big jerks that day." She winked. "I'm happy to see you've formed a friendship. I'd hate to have to break up another fight between you."

Shane elbowed Raul in the belly. "Yeah, who knew Raul liked fishing as much as I do?"

"We wouldn't have known if that grassfire hadn't nearly destroyed his home and his boat parked beside it." Raul shook his head. "The Lord works in mysterious ways."

"How did your ex take the news of your engagement?" Chance asked Rider.

"Her father let us know she took it better than he expected," Rider's mother said. "Apparently, her rehab is going well. She's been off the hard drugs for a few weeks, and is learning how to cope with her anger issues."

"That's nice of her father to give you an update on his daughter," Kinsey said.

"He felt awful about what Lydia did to Selena," Rider said.

"And how she destroyed Rider's garage," Selena added.

"He's paying to rebuild the garage and the apartment over it. He also paid to have Lola's garage painted, inside and out," Rider said.

Shane's brow dipped. "Your ex tried to talk me into burning down your garage. I told that crazy bit —woman where she could go with that idea."

"When is Lydia's court date?" Beckett asked. Kinsey perched at the foot of the lounge he'd sprawled out on.

"Three months, if her attorney doesn't get the date moved again," Selena said.

"How's the new shop coming along?" Shane asked.

"Should be finished by the time Selena heads off to school." Rider slipped an arm around Selena's waist and kissed the top of her hair.

"I'm going to miss you," Selena said and wrapped her arms around his waist.

"I'll come to visit as much as you can stand me," Rider promised.

"Then you might as well move in with me." Selena smiled up at him.

Rider shook his head. "You'll need your time to focus on your studies. I promise not to get in the way of you reaching your full potential." He brushed a strand of hair away from her cheek. "Don't worry, I'll be here in Hellfire when you come home. Just promise me one thing."

"What's that?"

"Don't forget to come home."

She hugged him around the middle and pressed her cheek against his chest. "I won't forget. Home is where the heart is. And my heart belongs to you."

HELLFIRE IN HIGH HEELS

HELLFIRE SERIES BOOK #4

New York Times & USA Today
Bestselling Author

ELLE JAMES

Hellfire In
Highheels

A HELLFIRE STORY

ELLE JAMES

NEW YORK TIMES BESTSELLING AUTHOR

CHAPTER 1

Lola Engel flipped the sign in the window of her shoe shop to display CLOSED and exited the building, pulling the door shut behind her. She locked it and glanced at her watch.

Damn.

She had only an hour to get home, change and stage an "accident" before Chance Grayson went off duty at the fire station.

Running in high heels was never good, nor classy. If at all possible, Lola avoided running in public. Scarred as a child by name-calling bullies, she didn't want anyone comparing her to an epileptic giraffe during a grand mal seizure. So, she hurried, skipping along, and then running all out when she verified no one was watching.

For a thirty-nine-year-old woman—okay, forty-three, though no one but her doctor knew the truth

—she kept her body in top physical condition, with not an ounce of fat on her thighs or belly. Since her husband had passed, she'd had loads of time on her hands. Time she preferred to fill working out or flirting with the best-looking man in Hellfire, Texas.

Chance Grayson. One of the four Grayson brothers, all of whom were incredibly clean-cut, drool-worthy, butt-hugging, jean-clad cowboys and fire-fighters. They'd struck it rich in the gene pool, and Lola wouldn't mind having some of that gold stretched out in her bed.

Oh, she wasn't looking for long-term commitment or love. She'd already been in love once and losing someone you cared for as much as she'd cared for Mr. Engel hurt far too much.

No, she'd vowed to enjoy an active sex life with whomever the hell she pleased, and screw the tongue-wagging, back-stabbing biddies of the community who thought they were better than anyone else because they were married and settled.

Settled only meant living in a rut. Lola refused to slip on a ring or into a rut. Losing her husband had taught her one valuable lesson: *Life was too damned short.* She had to seize it by the balls and hold on to that orgasmic finish line.

Two blocks down, two to go. Why the hell had she walked to work that morning? And why the hell hadn't she worn tennis shoes?

Because you're too goddamn vain and won't let others

see you in anything less than the most expensive shoes this side of the Mississippi.

New York City didn't have anything on Hellfire, Texas. Lola made damn sure of that. If she didn't sell many expensive shoes in her brick-and-mortar store, she sold a truckload every week from her online shop.

Just because a person lived in small-town, snail's-paced Texas didn't mean a woman had to deprive herself of the best and sexiest shoes from some of the most fabulous designers this world had to offer.

Slowly, but surely, she'd educated the ranchers' wives on the difference between Jimmy Choos stilet-toes and Ariat cowboy boots. Not many of the wives had the kind of money for the more expensive brands, but Lola stocked budget knock-offs to satisfy the locals.

At that moment, she would trade her Jimmy Choos for some running shoes. All because she wanted a shot at seducing Chance Grayson. The younger man had caught her eye the day she'd seen him shirtless hosing down his big, red fire truck.

The day had been a typical hotter-than-Hades summer one in Texas. Sweat had glistened on the young man's shoulders, and all Lola could think was how she wanted to run her hands over every part of Chance's body. Then she'd start all over with her tongue.

Who said a woman of thirty-nine had to settle for

men her own age? Forty-year-old men dated twenty-somethings all the time. Lola was a heck of a lot better in bed than most of those little girls. She could show Chance Grayson a thing or two. She just had to get his attention.

ABOUT THE AUTHOR

ELLE JAMES also writing as MYLA JACKSON is a
New York Times and *USA Today* Bestselling author of
books including cowboys, intrigues and paranormal
adventures that keep her readers on the edges of
their seats. With over eighty works in a variety of
sub-genres and lengths she has published with
Harlequin, Samhain, Ellora's Cave, Kensington, Cleis
Press, and Avon. When she's not at her computer,
she's traveling, snow skiing, boating, or riding her
ATV, dreaming up new stories. Learn more about
Elle James at www.ellejames.com

Website | Facebook | Twitter | GoodReads |
Newsletter | BookBub | Amazon

Or visit her alter ego Myla Jackson at
mylajackson.com
Website | Facebook | Twitter | Newsletter

Follow Me!
www.ellejames.com
ellejames@ellejames.com